"You're ⬚⬚⬚⬚⬚⬚⬚⬚⬚, Maggie."

Chase knotted the towel around his waist. "I want you so bad my teeth ache. Do you want me back?" He stared at her with hot intensity. "Say something, dammit."

For a sizzling moment, she met his gaze. Yes, she wanted him—but did she have the guts to act on it?

She sucked in a breath. "There must be something in the air tonight because I feel…"

He stepped toward her, the towel now riding dangerously low on his hips. "It's not in the air—it's in the blood." He reached for her. "Beautiful, beautiful Maggie. There's so much I want to say to you…do to you…do for you."

"Then drop that silly towel," she said in a strangled voice, "and *show* me, Chase. Just this once, before I lose my nerve."

The towel hit the tiles.

Dear Reader,

I'm in love with the American West and the entire Western myth. I could never resist a story about strong, handsome cowboys and beautiful, feisty cowgirls. When I began writing stories of my own, I became even more caught up in the Western mystique.

The natural result was a miniseries for Harlequin in 1993 about the Taggarts of Texas. Since several of my formative years were spent in the Lone Star State, I relished the opportunity to write the kind of books I love to read.

When I moved to the Centennial State a while back, it quickly became apparent that Texas and Colorado are "the same, only different." Both have lots of cows, cowboys and cowgirls, and some of the finest and friendliest people on earth. Other than weather, the biggest difference I noticed was that the only Coloradans who say "y'all" are transplanted Texans.

Naturally, I found another Western miniseries evolving from new surroundings and experiences: a May Day snowstorm, a trip over Independence Pass with my heart in my mouth, a swim in the world's largest hot-springs pool at Glenwood Springs…and the exploits of an old gray mare renowned as an escape artist.

All these adventures and discoveries—and many more—ended up in the three Camerons of Colorado books about a ranching family chock-full of rugged individuals. I hope you'll enjoy the stories of Ben, Maggie and Julie, and then…who knows where my love of the West will lead?

Maybe… Hey, maybe Thom T. Taggart of Texas and Etta May Cameron of Colorado ought to get together! Or what about—

Sincerely,

Ruth Jean Dale

THE CUPID CONSPIRACY
Ruth Jean Dale

Harlequin Books

TORONTO • NEW YORK • LONDON
AMSTERDAM • PARIS • SYDNEY • HAMBURG
STOCKHOLM • ATHENS • TOKYO • MILAN
MADRID • WARSAW • BUDAPEST • AUCKLAND

For Elnora (AKA Nogy) and Captain Hoek
with all kinds of love and appreciation

ISBN 0-373-25679-5

THE CUPID CONSPIRACY

Copyright © 1996 by Betty Duran

1

MAGGIE CAMERON COLBY stared up at the black-and-chrome-and-glass restaurant. The place was tucked back in the trees on a Colorado mountainside overlooking Aspen and the Roaring Fork Valley. A discreet sign across the tall double doors murmured, rather than shouted, the immodest name of the establishment: Chase Britton's.

He'd named it after himself. Didn't it just figure? Maggie clenched her teeth, feeling her preconceived notions justified.

She didn't want to be here. When her brother Ben and his wife, Betsy, invited her to tag along to Aspen for supplies, she should have turned them down cold. She'd known that Betsy would naturally suggest lunch at the restaurant of her old friend, Chase Britton. But Maggie had counted on persuading them to drop her off at a bookstore first, and this they'd declined to do.

So here she was, about to enter the lair of the man responsible for—

"You comin', Maggie?"

Ben waited, door held open and Betsy already disappearing inside. It was too late now. Maggie would just have to brazen it out.

As A MERE LAD of seven some thirty years ago, Chase Britton made an amazing discovery: not everybody loved him. This unwelcome revelation was provided by a young lady of similar years, the daughter of a supplier used by his father's chain of restaurants.

Confidently Chase had given the girl his most winning smile, the one that, even at his tender age, got him just about anything he wanted.

She'd given *him* a fat lip, employing a lethal right that filled him with admiration even as the taste of blood filled his mouth.

Her father had yelled at her, but the damage was done; Chase had met rejection up close and personal. His first impulse had been to return tit for tat, but his own father would have done more than simply yell. In the Britton family, boys didn't hit girls, period. End of discussion.

So Chase had licked the blood from his lip and kept right on smiling. Instead of decking this pint-size female terrorist, he'd said the first thing that popped into his head: "I'll let you ride my pony if you promise not to hurt him."

After that, she'd been putty in his hands.

So why did he think of that girl, whose name he didn't even remember, every time he was forced by circumstances to spend a few interminable minutes with Margaret Colby? Maggie hadn't taken a swing at him yet, but he figured it was just a matter of time. Hell, if it'd loosen her up, he'd *give* her a damn pony.

Initially Chase had welcomed the arrival of the Camerons, since they'd interrupted yet another scene with his twelve-year-old daughter, Blair. Ever the gracious host, he'd insisted they join him for a festive lunch—on the house of course.

Festive? Maybe if he stood on his head and whistled "Dixie."

Still, he felt duty-bound to do his best. Pouring expensive champagne for all, he offered a glass to Maggie, along with a smile he was confident she wouldn't be able to tell from the real thing. She'd already cast a jaundiced eye upon the decor and the menu. Now she peered at the sparkling wine as if she thought he intended to poison her.

She hadn't changed since the last time he'd seen her, in Betsy's Rusty Spur Café in the little Colorado mountain town whimsically named Cupid. Maggie was as frumpy and hostile as ever. He presumed that when she opened her mouth, she'd also prove to be the same sharp-tongued shrew he remembered only too well.

There weren't many people he couldn't get along with. Unfortunately two of them—Maggie Colby and his daughter, Blair—were sitting at the table with him now. Blair, from a child's perspective, had reason to resent him. Maggie might *think* she did, but their "misunderstanding" was her doing, not his. What kind of convoluted thinking had led her to conclude otherwise?

He studied her without seeming to do so. Stern and humorless, she wore her dark hair slicked away from an oval face, which made her look even less appealing. That face, with its high cheekbones and smooth olive skin, was habitually devoid of expression—except for the eyes. The rich brown of fine chocolate, her eyes revealed a lively intelligence spoiled, in his opinion, by a grating superiority; her very composure irritated him.

She was also a hypocrite, which irritated him more.

When she lifted her champagne flute toward light streaming through a glass wall, he—easygoing, good-natured Chase Britton—was braced for anything.

"Cleopatra's melted pearls—on a Wednesday yet," she said in a faintly censorious tone. "You shouldn't have, you know."

Byron, huh? Chase kept on smiling. "But we're celebrating a milestone," he protested mildly, "our first encounter on *my* turf. Champagne is the only appropriate way to salute beginnings."

She sipped. "Or seal endings—treaties, careers, contracts. Deaths."

She might be joking; Chase was never sure with Maggie. "It does make the mundane seem special." He tried to keep his jaw from grinding too noticeably. Since that first meeting almost four years ago, he'd been subjected to her prickly company on only a few occasions—although curiously enough, he'd never met her husband. Poor guy must have his hands full.

Maggie had riled him to the point where he'd practically forgotten they weren't alone at the table—not that he'd screwed up his schedule to host this impromptu luncheon for *her* sake. He'd done it for Betsy, a friend from his California days long before she'd married Maggie's rancher brother, Ben.

Betsy's smile looked a bit anxious. "To beginnings. Personally I adore champagne anytime day or night." She took a sip.

Chase nodded absent agreement, trying not to glare at Maggie. She'd hurt his feelings with her caustic remark. He gave her his most unctuous smile. "The wine doesn't meet with your approval? Perhaps a different vintage—I'll call the steward."

"Please don't bother." Her gaze remained cool.

"But you don't seem to be enjoying it."

"Doubtless because I learned to drink champagne on five-dollar-a-bottle stuff. I'm afraid that's my standard of measurement."

Chase choked on the hundred-dollar-a-bottle stuff in his glass. So much for impressing the prickly Maggie—not that he'd been trying. Reaching for a linen napkin, he decided she was putting him on. Wasn't she?

His daughter shifted restlessly in her chair, her expression dour. Chase wished—too late—that he hadn't insisted Blair come along to lunch. Storm clouds gathered in her face.

The girl leaned forward with her elbows on the table, staring insolently at Ben. "So what are *you* supposed to be?" she demanded. "A cowboy or something?"

Ben looked startled. He glanced down at his blue-plaid Western shirt, then back at the girl, whose impertinent expression was unrelenting.

As her father, Chase felt obliged to do *something*, so he said, "That was rude, Blair." Damn, he sounded resigned, not authoritative. But ever since she'd moved to Aspen, they'd been at odds over just about everything. She was wearing him down.

Ben looked amused. "No problem." He said to Blair, "I'm a rancher. Ranchers are cowboys, but not all cowboys are ranchers."

Blair frowned. "Is that a riddle? If it is, I don't want to play."

"Blair!" Chase glanced around the table apologetically.

Betsy smiled at Blair. "It was an honest question. What would Blair know about ranchers? She's new to Colorado." She added brightly, "So how do you like Aspen, honey?"

"I don't," Blair shot back, "but I don't have much choice, do I? I'd rather be in New York with my mother, but *he* won't let me." She glared at her father.

Betsy's smile never faltered. "I'm sure you'll love Aspen when you get to know it better," she said staunchly, "and the rest of Colorado, too."

Blair drooped in her chair. "The whole state stinks."

Maggie, directly across the table from Blair, toyed with a salad fork while she watched the exchange. Wisps of dark hair had escaped the single fat braid dangling down her back, softening the austere lines of her face. "Didn't you know that we live on a ranch?" she asked the girl.

"I knew *she* did." Blair glanced resentfully at Betsy.

"We all do," Maggie said, "along with our grandmother, and Ben and Betsy's three kids, and my younger brother and sister, who are twins. It's a real ranch with horses and cows and dogs—you name it."

"Bears?" Blair asked.

Maggie cast an amused glance at Betsy. "Yes. And mountain lions and deer and beavers and—"

"Yeah, yeah, I get it—out in the middle of nowhere." Blair's smile was sheepish. "So what's your point?"

"Just that maybe you'd like to visit someday. The Straight Arrow Ranch really is a neat place." Maggie's voice had lost its usual sarcastic edge and sounded warmly encouraging. "We'd love to have you."

Chase held his breath, surprised and pleased. In the five months his daughter had been with him, she'd shown little interest in anything or anybody. He wouldn't have been surprised if she'd laughed in Maggie's face.

Instead, she shrugged. "I don't care," she said. "It's up to *him*. We do what *he* wants to do."

Ben made a great show of thumping a hand upon the table, but he was grinning. "That's the way it should be," he declared. "Kids should be seen and not—"

Betsy jammed an elbow in her husband's ribs, cutting off the rest of it. And then the waiter appeared, and the wine steward and soon the chef. But even in that flurry of activity, Chase clung to the realization that Blair had given Maggie a definite maybe.

Which was more than he'd been able to drag from her on any occasion to date.

MAGGIE STOOD before the floor-to-ceiling mirror in the ladies' room, the dramatic theatrical lighting revealing her every flaw. Frowning, she smoothed the escaping wisps of hair back into the braid hanging between her shoulder blades. Her hair was her only vanity: long, thick, dark as night and crackling with vitality. But because she considered vanity a waste of time in a woman of her age and circumstance—a thirty-five-year-old widow, totally lacking in sex appeal—she wore her hair in a severe style that downplayed her finest feature.

She wouldn't want the obnoxiously self-confident Chase Britton to think she was trying to entice him with her nonexistent sex appeal. She knew to her grief that he was an expert at jumping to conclusions.

Just then the washroom door swung open to admit Blair, putting a stop to Maggie's brooding. The girl had an adolescent awkwardness that Maggie found greatly appealing, despite the petulance and abominable manners. She liked children in general, and this girl in particular. There was something about her that seemed almost...wounded, as if she'd suffered more than a girl of her age and situation should have. Blair halted, head cocked and hands clasped behind her back.

She wore khaki shorts and a plain yellow T-shirt, with klunky leather sandals on sun-browned feet, all with the flair that said "money."

She was also twelve or thirteen. If life were fair, Maggie would have a child about that age.

"You have pretty hair," Blair announced, rocking back on her heels.

Maggie smiled. "Thanks. So do you."

Blair's hand flew to her sleek brown bob. "I hate it. It's so *straight*."

"And thick and shiny."

For a moment, their glances met and held. Then Blair let out her breath in an explosive grunt. "So. How come you don't like him?"

That shrewd observation startled Maggie. "Don't like who?" she said, stalling, knowing perfectly well.

Blair seemed willing to play along. "My father. Don't worry, you can say it. I don't like him much, either."

The girl's comments put Maggie squarely on the horns of a dilemma. She could lie or she could tell the truth. If she lied, she suspected Blair would recognize it for what it was. She acted like a girl who'd been lied to plenty. Had it been by her father?

Maggie knew only the sketchiest of details about the Brittons, father and daughter: Blair's parents had been divorced for years, and the girl had been living with her mother in another state; recently Betsy had mentioned Blair's moving into her father's Aspen home.

Why the switch in custodial arrangements, Maggie didn't know, nor did she consider it her business. She *did* consider it her business to be as candid as she could with this unhappy child.

So she responded carefully. "I'm not too crazy about your father, that's true, but sometimes people just don't click. That doesn't mean they're not good people or there's anything wrong with either of them, it just means the . . . the . . ."

"Chemistry?" Blair offered, straight-faced.

Maggie laughed. "What does a kid your age know about chemistry?"

"I'm precocious." Blair lifted her chin, but her eyes gleamed with humor. "I know plenty."

"Maybe not as much as you think. I suggest—"

"If you're going to bawl me out . . ."

"Certainly not."

"What, then?"

"A word to the wise, okay?"

Blair hesitated. "Okay," she agreed cautiously.

"I don't know what's eating you and I'm not asking, since I'm in no position to do anything about it. But you've been . . . less than gracious since we got here. I don't know what you hope to accomplish, but if it's to make your father look bad, give it up. All you're doing is making *yourself* look bad. I'm sorry if that's harsh, but it's true."

Blair's face tightened but didn't crumble; the girl was made of stronger stuff than that. "What am I *supposed* to do?" she exploded. "I don't see any reason why I should be nice to him when he *forced* me to come here."

Uh-oh, Maggie thought. *Chase Britton, you've got trouble.* "Be that as it may, you can catch more flies with honey than with vinegar."

"I don't want to catch flies!"

"You want *something*. If you ever expect to get it, you're on the wrong track. Being rude, upsetting your father, isn't going to make you happy. All it'll do is make you miserable—more miserable."

"That's not fair!"

"Welcome to real life. Some things you can fight and some you can't." Maggie patted the stiff shoulder. "You're a bright girl, Blair. Nothing good will ever come from being rude to perfectly well-meaning strangers. Think!" Maggie tapped a forefinger against the girl's temple.

"Think?" Blair blinked.

"Piece of cake for a smart cookie like you."

That drew a reluctant smile. But as they walked together down the silver-carpeted hallway to the dining room, Maggie thought about the advice she'd given this girl, whom she hardly knew. *Don't do as I do*, she thought with a touch of irony. *Do as I say.*

Thank heaven she herself wasn't involved with the Brittons. She didn't want to be involved in anything that concerned *him*. The man was, as her grandma would say, trouble on the hoof.

Seated once more, Maggie considered Chase Britton as dispassionately as her disapproval would allow. He was, bluntly stated, drop-dead gorgeous—right away, a reason for a plain Jane to be wary. His dark hair was streaked with an attractive silver at the temples, although he was only thirty-seven—a sleek, hard-muscled thirty-seven. His features were finely etched, yet intensely masculine. But it was his eyes, a clear light hazel, that intrigued Maggie in spite of herself. In them she could see a man so sure of himself, of his charm and his place in the universe, that nothing and no one stood a chance against him.

Except possibly one sullen young girl; certainly not a country bumpkin like Maggie Colby.

He might be an old friend of Betsy's, but he'd never be a friend of Maggie's. She wouldn't trust him as far as she could throw him. His daughter was probably on the right track, after all.

EXCUSED FROM THE TABLE at last, a subdued and thoughtful Blair said graceful goodbyes and departed. Chase watched her go, his expression bewildered. "I don't get it," he said. "What came over her? And where can I buy a ton of it?"

Betsy nodded sympathetically. "How long has she been with you, Chase?"

"Five months, and the last ten minutes was the best part." He shoved his hands through the silver wings of hair. "I'm at my wit's end, Betts. She's rude, she's defiant, she's . . . miserable, and I don't know what to do about it. She's also a bright girl, yet she failed most of her sixth-grade classes. I've got to hire a tutor to work with her over the summer, and I haven't been able to come up with anyone she'll accept."

Ben snorted, his disdain coming through loud and clear—but then, Maggie knew that Ben would run his home like a military boot camp if Betsy let him. Maggie could almost see the thought forming in Betsy's mind: *What a coincidence! Maggie's a teacher.*

Maggie rushed in, forestalling her sister-in-law. "Don't you think we'd better get going? We still have to stop at that restaurant-supply store and a bookstore before we head home."

Betsy leaned forward eagerly. "But Maggie, you're a—"

"It's time to go, Betsy." Maggie's tone was quelling enough for Betsy to get the hint. She stood up and, unable to resist a last shot at Chase, added, "Thank you so much for everything—wine, food, company. Dining with you has certainly been . . . interesting."

He picked up the gauntlet. "Only interesting? You disappoint me, Maggie. Why, the first time I met you—"

"Forget the first time we met." She smiled sweetly and told a bare-faced lie: "I have."

BETSY LET the whole thing slide until they'd finished their shopping and were heading back to Cupid through Independence Pass. Then she shifted around to look curiously at Maggie, buckled into the back while Ben drove.

"So what was that all about?"

"All what?" Maggie closed one of the books she'd bought in Aspen, a new history of Colorado. The thing she disliked most about her little hometown was the dearth of bookstores. If you couldn't buy it at the grocery or the drugstore, you weren't going to find it in Cupid—and among the missing was almost everything that interested Maggie. She'd just dropped more than a hundred dollars on books, a hundred dollars she could ill afford but nevertheless didn't regret spending.

What was life without books? Hardly worth living, in her opinion. Her financial situation was so dire that a hundred bucks wasn't going to make much difference, anyway.

Betsy persisted. "I'm talking about your not letting me tell Chase you're a teacher."

"I don't want to be Blair's tutor."

"I don't see why not. You'd be perfect."

"Nobody's perfect."

"You would be for this. Why don't you want to tutor her? You like her and—"

"I like all kids or I wouldn't be a teacher. But maybe I don't want to spend my summer doing the same thing I've been doing for the past nine months."

"You don't have to get testy." Betsy frowned. "Look, Maggie, it's no secret in the family that you need to make some money—"

"And no secret in town, either. But I've already got a job, or have you forgotten? I'll be waiting tables at the Rusty Spur again this summer."

Betsy frowned. "What'll you make waitressing in our little bitty ol' café? You'd make a lot more working for Chase. You know you're more than qualified."

"True, but—"

"And you need the money."

"Also true, but—"

"And the prospect of spending the summer in Aspen shouldn't be all that shabby."

"Would be to me," Ben cut in, slowing for another of the interminable hairpin curves leading up to the twelve-thousand-foot summit of the pass.

"Nobody's asking you," Betsy said tartly to her husband before turning back to her sister-in-law. "You've got nothing against Aspen, have you?"

"No, but if you'll just let me get a word in edgewise..."

Betsy clamped her lips together and nodded.

"There's one small problem."

"Which is?"

"I absolutely detest Chase Britton."

Betsy's mouth dropped open. "Why on earth would...? Chase is wonderful! He's loyal and trustworthy and rich and well educated—and not too hard on the eyes, either. What's not to like?"

"Okay, you asked." Maggie realized she'd have to be careful what she said on this subject, since Betsy was prejudiced in his favor. "That first time Chase came to Cupid, he was trying to hit on you. Naturally I didn't like it, since we were all working so hard to get you and this pigheaded brother of mine together."

"No way!"

"Betsy, I don't know how you can be so naive. Maybe you were so besotted with Ben by then you didn't see what was going on."

"Shh!" Betsy laid a finger across pursed lips. "We don't want Ben to get a big head."

"Too late!" Maggie grinned at the back of her brother's head. "That's when I discovered Mr. Chase Britton is a conceited jerk."

"Hmm. Did something happen I don't know about?"

"We...had words. The few times I've seen him since have done nothing to alter that first impression. So why would I want to work for him, I ask you?"

"Because," Ben growled, "you need the money."

"I don't need it *that* badly. Besides, Cupid's too far away to commute, and by the time I paid for a place to stay, there wouldn't be any profit left. You know how Aspen prices are."

"That's true," Betsy conceded. "But Maggie, he really is a very nice—"

"*Last but not least*, he hasn't offered me the job."

Betsy brightened. "Probably because he doesn't know you're a teacher."

"Let's keep it that way." Maggie gave Betsy one of those looks that effectively closed any discussion among the Camerons of Cupid, Colorado.

THEY REACHED the ranch house just in time for supper, receiving a big welcome from Ben and Betsy's children, Lisa Marie and Joey, seven and eight respectively, and two-year-old Catherine. The kids were trailed by Roger and Erica, Lisa Marie's cat and dog, plus Joey's mutt, Killer.

Julie, Maggie's younger sister, arrived home shortly afterward from her job at Cupid's small weekly newspaper, and added her voice to the usual bedlam. Everyone talked and vied for attention at once, while Grandma Cameron, from her position at the stove, smiled and occasionally waved a wooden spoon, warning that supper would be on the table any minute.

Despite the size of the mob, two faces were missing. Jason, Julie's twin, would return eventually; he was in Texas or Oklahoma or Wyoming competing in some rodeo. He'd gone on the circuit almost three years ago, just as he'd always dreamed of doing. Now twenty-five, he was hitting his stride and had hopes of making the national finals in Las Vegas this year. He'd be back home for a visit one of these days.

The other missing face was that of Maggie's husband. Chuck Colby had died thirteen months ago, at least technically. In actual fact, he'd been dying by inches for a long time before that.

A truck driver when he and Maggie married, he'd spent all but a pitifully few months of their marriage in a wheelchair, the result of a fiery freeway crash. She'd watched her big happy husband shrivel away until he'd become a mere shell of his former lusty self. Fighting constant pain, he'd looked upon death as a deliverance. It had come to him cradled in her arms, in the bedroom they'd shared here at the Straight Arrow Ranch.

Sometimes Maggie felt she should have died with him, since she seemed to have forgotten how to live during those years devoted to his care. Her social skills were nil. Her career as an educator was in disarray, for she'd been reduced to substitute teaching and had neither the tenure nor the seniority her age and experience warranted.

But besides missing Chuck and feeling so horribly guilty because he was gone and she was still alive, she'd been left with crushing medical bills. Ben had offered to help; so had Granny. Even Jason and Julie, never noted for thrift, had gone to Maggie, separately and together, trying to press their meager savings on her.

She'd turned them down as gently as she could, knowing she must keep her pride since it was about all she had left. Chuck had been *her* husband, and she would pay their debts. The family had already done more than enough, rearranging their lives to welcome Chuck and Maggie into the fold when they'd had nowhere else to turn. She'd taken too much from them already.

When she walked into the big kitchen for supper that night, she was hardly surprised to find three ominous-looking envelopes had come for her in the day's mail. She didn't need to open them; she knew what they contained. She would pay something on each bill as soon as she started summer work at the Rusty Spur, the café owned by Betsy and Betsy's aunt Nancy. Maggie laid the envelopes aside, aware that Granny and Betsy watched with sympathetic expressions.

After the meal, after the kitchen was cleaned, after the children were tucked into bed and the animals evicted and Ben retired to the family room with his journals, Betsy marched to the telephone on the wall and dialed. Maggie, pad of paper before her on the table and pencil poised, about to go over the financial numbers yet again, felt only mild curiosity until she heard Betsy say Chase Britton's name.

2

MAGGIE'S PENCIL clattered to the floor, earning her a curious glance from Granny.

Betsy deliberately turned her back to her audience and spoke softly. "Chase? I know it must be a surprise to hear from me so soon . . . thank you, we had a wonderful time, too. Say, I've been thinking, you know, about you and Blair coming to visit the Straight Arrow?"

She hesitated; she laughed and nodded. "Yes, Maggie's invitation still stands. We'd love to have you . . . Uh-huh, how about Saturday? Yes, this Saturday! Blair will love it here. . . . Just drive straight through Cupid to the north until . . ."

As Betsy gave directions, Maggie sat at the kitchen table doing a slow boil. She knew what Betsy was up to and didn't like it one bit. When her sister-in-law hung up the phone, Maggie was ready.

"I don't want you volunteering me to tutor Chase Britton's daughter, okay?"

Betsy just stood there, a thoughtful expression on her face. No wonder Chase had pursued her, Maggie thought irritably. They'd have been a perfect match, both beautiful people born with silver spoons in their mouths. How Betsy and Ben ever got together was still a mystery to her.

"Not okay," Betsy said.

Maggie blinked in surprise. She couldn't remember Betsy ever refusing any even halfway reasonable request. "Darn it, Betsy," Maggie began, "you don't know—"

Grandma Cameron intervened. "Give it a rest, Maggie." She pursed her lips. Despite her advanced years—eighty-plus, but she declined to be specific— Etta May had a remarkably unlined face, and gray eyes as shrewd as they'd ever been. "Betsy's explained the situation to me, and I don't think you should say no until you give it more thought. Sounds to me like that little girl needs you, and heaven only knows, you need the money."

"Good grief!" Maggie slumped in her chair. "You two have it all figured out, and *he* doesn't even know I'm a teacher! When he does, he's not going to offer me the job for a zillion reasons, the most important being that he doesn't like me any more than I like him."

"Izzat so?" Granny sounded unconvinced.

"Yes, it's so."

"No, it's not," Betsy put in firmly. "What's the *real* reason you're so opposed to this, Maggie?"

"I told you, I detest the man. I don't trust him." Maggie stood and gathered up her papers and pencils. "But he's your friend, Betsy. I'll say nothing more against him—unless you force me. I appreciate what you're trying to do, but my answer is no. No, no, thank you very much but no!"

Stalking from the room, she heard Granny remark, "Methinks the lady doth protest too much."

Damn that Shakespeare.

THE CLOSER THEY GOT to the Straight Arrow Ranch, the more excited Blair became, although Chase could see her trying to hide it. He could hardly believe this was the same sullen girl who'd dragged herself to breakfast a few hours earlier.

"Is it much farther?" she demanded for the fourth or fifth time. Bouncing impatiently in her bucket seat, she looked through the window of the Jaguar just as it glided past the Hideout, a honky-tonk on the southern edge of Cupid.

Chase had vivid memories of the Hideout, although he'd only been there once and that several years ago. It was the company that made it so memorable: Betsy and her then soon-to-be sisters-in-law, Maggie and Julie.

Hell, he hadn't known until after the fact that the Cameron sisters had been trying to set Betsy up with their taciturn brother, Ben. Chase's unexpected appearance had throw a minor crimp into their plans, but it had all worked out. He'd even laughed about it later with Julie.

Not with Maggie, though. Maggie apparently didn't know how to laugh; smiling was a stretch for her. She took everything with deadly seriousness, an unattractive trait to a man who took almost nothing seriously.

Her husband, Chase had concluded, was welcome to her.

"Want to stop at that drive-in up there for a cold drink before we go on?" he asked Blair, the original Junk Food Kid. He was trying to wean her from burgers and fries and tacos, but a lemonade wouldn't be out of order. He slowed the car.

"Don't stop!"

"Huh?"

She hung her head sheepishly. "Just keep going, okay? I . . . I don't want to be late."

"No, of course not." He stifled his smile and drove through and on out of town; blink your eyes and you could miss it.

Blair glanced at him, then away. "Do you think they'll really let me ride a horse?"

"I suspect they'll insist on it," he said dryly, knowing the tendency of Westerners to shove everybody on a horse. Especially a tenderfoot, and preferably on an animal called Buttercup, when Dynamite would have been more appropriate.

They wouldn't try anything on Blair, though; women and children came in for special consideration. The Camerons were welcome to try anything they liked on him—hell, he looked forward to it. Chase was a native Coloradan, although the spoon in his mouth had been just as silver as they all doubtless suspected.

But he hadn't grown up a hothouse flower. His father, today a hale and hearty sixty-seven and head of the Britton chain of twenty-seven gourmet restaurants worldwide, had made sure his only son learned how to take care of himself. For six years beginning when he was twelve, Chase had spent summers working at a cattle ranch in Montana, earning his keep and doing a man's work—although his father's motives originally might have been less than altruistic. Eight months after the death of Chase's mother, the elder Britton had taken up with a Las Vegas showgirl.

Chloe was, in her lover's words, "a good old broad," although at first he didn't consider her fit company for his impressionable son. But appearances could be maintained for only so long, and eventually Chase got to know his father's paramour.

He quickly grew to share his father's assessment; Chloe *was* a good old broad, generous and kind without being judgmental.

Even after Chloe was no longer a stranger to Chase, the ranch working vacations continued, ending only when Chase went away to college. He'd never forgotten the lessons he'd learned on the range, lessons about loyalty and trust and fair play.

Slowing the car, he looked for the dirt-road turnoff Betsy had described, since he'd never been to the ranch before. *Hit me with your best shot, Camerons*, he thought with a trace of smugness. He wouldn't mind looking good in front of his daughter.

An unpaved road opened up to the left, and he whipped the Jag into a turn and drove straight into the heart of some of the most beautiful mountain scenery Colorado—or the world—had to offer.

Twenty minutes later the Jag glided to a stop before the ranch house where Betsy and the kids waited on the steps. She'd never looked better, Chase thought admiringly. The marriage was obviously a great success.

She greeted him with a kiss on the cheek. Together they stood for a moment, watching Betsy's kids coax Blair to the corral where Ben was already saddling up.

Chase returned Ben's wave, then shook his head in amazement. "I can't believe how Lisa Marie's grown," he said, stunned at the changes he saw in Betsy's daughter. Last time he'd seen the girl, she'd been an extremely precocious five-year-old. Unfortunately he was able to touch base with Betsy and her family only infrequently, for they all led busy lives. Now he saw that at seven, Lisa had lost that appealing baby precocity and showed a maturity beyond her years.

"They do grow up fast, don't they." With a sigh, Betsy took his arm. "She loves it here, and so do I. Let's go inside so you can say hello to the rest of the family."

A curly-haired toddler ran to meet them at the door. Betsy scooped the child into her arms and nuzzled the chubby cheek. "This is Cat, short for Catherine. Say hello to the nice man, Cat."

"No!" Cat smiled angelically. "Hello, man."

Something clamped down hard around Chase's heart. He could remember Blair at about this age running into his arms. His daughter had adored him then, although she didn't remember it now.

Sometimes he wished he didn't remember it, either.

Betsy stood the child on her feet. "Oh, the terrible twos!" She straightened with a rueful smile, then spotted her sister-in-law. "Maggie, Chase is here."

"So I see," Maggie said.

Chase ignored her less-than-effusive greeting, merely dipping his head in solemn acknowledgment. Maggie wore jeans and boots like the rest of the family, and a sloppy shirt that might have been her husband's or brother's. In fact, now that he thought about it, she always seemed to wear clothing that concealed her body. Which led him to wonder what might be wrong with it.

Julie approached then, her arm around the waist of a preppy-looking young man. "Howdy, stranger!" Julie winked at Chase, her brown eyes sparkling with mischief. "This is Rick Michaels, my fiancé."

"Pleased to meet you," Chase said, and stuck out his hand.

Rick took it and said, "Likewise."

Betsy smiled at the tall stern-looking old lady who'd appeared in a doorway. "I believe you met Grandma Cameron at my wedding. Granny, you remember my friend, Chase Britton? His daughter, Blair, is running around outside with the rest of the kids."

"Ma'am." Chase inclined his head in a gesture of respect. "I'm pleased to see you again."

Etta May grinned broadly, the sternness melting away. Chase found himself thinking Maggie should try it someday.

"My stars," Granny said, "you do have fine manners! I've heard a lot about you, young man, and you're heartily welcome at the Straight Arrow. Now I gotta get back to my kitchen, or this picnic won't never get off the ground!"

She wheeled and disappeared back the way she'd come.

Betsy watched the old lady with obvious affection, then turned to Chase. "That's the crew, all except Jason. He's off getting his bones broken and his brains knocked out at some rodeo."

Chase glanced at Maggie. "But I thought . . . ?"

Betsy glanced at him quickly. "You didn't know about Chuck?"

"Chuck?"

"My husband." Maggie's voice seemed uncommonly low. "I guess you never met him."

Chase shook his head.

"He died just over a year ago." Her lips tightened. "If you'll excuse me, I'll go give Granny a hand."

She walked into the kitchen, her back straight. Chase turned to Betsy. "I'm sorry. I didn't mean to be insensitive."

She shook her head. "You weren't. Did you know Chuck was a paraplegic?"

"No. No, I didn't." Well, he thought, that put a whole different slant on . . . a lot of things.

Betsy nodded. "He'd been in a wheelchair for years before I came here. Maggie took care of him for so long that, now he's gone, she's having a hard time adjusting. We—the whole family—feel she needs something to shake her out of her rut."

"Some ruts can get pretty comfortable," Chase suggested, thinking about himself as much as Maggie. Blair's coming to live with him had jarred him out of one of the most comfortable ruts a man could wish for. But Maggie's situation, well, that was rough.

Moments later Betsy led Chase outdoors into the mild June air, to a spot beneath an arbor just beginning to green up. From here they could oversee the goings-on in the corral, where Ben was teaching an eager Blair to ride. Laughter and an occasional word floated back to them. Chase felt an almost melancholy gratitude toward those who could make his unhappy daughter smile again.

"Chase."

Betsy sounded so serious he felt a flash of foreboding. "Yes?"

"Have you found a tutor for Blair yet?"

He grimaced. He was running out of time, not to mention applicants. For just one day, he'd hoped to avoid that nagging worry. "I'm trying," he said. "I've got a couple more interviews set for Monday, but I'm not optimistic."

"Cancel them," she said.

He raised his brows. "How so?"

"I know the perfect person for the job."

Suspicion crawled up his backbone. "Who?"

"Maggie."

He groaned. "I need a teacher, a real teacher, someone with experience."

"Maggie's a teacher. She was a regular at Cupid Elementary until she had to cut back to substitute status because of . . . you know, Chuck. She loves kids. It's a crime against nature that she doesn't have any of her own. But she *is* qualified, very much so."

"I'll take your word for it, but—"

"She'll be a wonderful role model for Blair," Betsy rushed on. "She's smart, well educated and of high moral character."

Chase was starting to sweat. "It's too far to commute."

Betsy laughed. "Go on, Chase, I've seen your house! You've got room for ten tutors if you wanted them."

"In my *house?* You want her to *live* with me?"

"No, silly, I want her to live with Blair. Think of her as a sort of governess. Then it won't seem so strange."

Frumpy, tart-tongued Maggie living in his house? Underfoot day and night?

"Look," he said desperately, "she wouldn't do it on a bet. I . . . make her nervous." Sounded better than saying, *She hates my guts.*

"Don't be ridiculous." Betsy sighed. "But even if that was a tiny bit true, she's crazy about Blair. Maggie felt some special connection to your daughter, Chase. Surely you saw it."

That dealt his defenses a blow from which they might not recover. "Let me think about this," he hedged.

"Fine." Betsy stood up. "Be thinking about the salary, too. Maggie's trying to pay off medical bills, and I think it'd be a good idea to make her an offer she can't refuse."

Ben followed Betsy toward the corral, wondering if she really expected him to put up with the generally disagreeable Maggie Colby for an entire summer and pay royally for the privilege. *Me, a man accustomed to more . . . malleable women.*

No. Hell, no. Not that there was a chance in a million that Maggie would go along with this cockamamy suggestion.

BLAIR WAS on her best behavior; in fact, her behavior was better than any best Chase had yet seen from her. She adored the horses, played willingly with the younger children, bounced Cat on her lap, petted the dog and cat and complimented Grandma Cameron on the food. She said "Yes, sir," and, "No, sir," to Ben, which was a sure way to win his approval, and laughed and giggled with Julie.

But if she liked the Camerons, she *adored* Maggie, who, Chase soon realized, returned the favor. To Maggie's credit, she didn't press, didn't pull, just let the girl come to her.

And Blair did. She sat next to Maggie for lunch at the picnic table beside the house, sought Maggie's approval and opinion on every subject, even talked Maggie into going riding with her after lunch so she could show off her new skills.

"Chase, why don't you join them?" Betsy suggested.

Maggie's brows flew up in quick alarm; she looked so unhappy at the prospect that Chase almost wished he *was* going. "I think I'll pass," he said dryly.

Ben shook his head solemnly. "Shame. We could've put you up on ol' Dobbin."

Aka Mankiller, Chase translated. Betsy had told him about this crazy bronc. "I hate to miss ol' Dobbin," he said with all sincerity, "but maybe Blair wants time away from her dad."

Everyone looked at Blair, who turned her head and began to babble to Maggie. "Your brother says I'll make a good rider if I can practice. He said I caught on as fast as anyone he ever taught, didn't you, Mr. Cameron? He says all I need now is mileage . . ."

Maggie glanced at Chase, quick compassion in her face as if she knew Blair had hurt him. She just didn't know how much.

Granny rose from the wooden picnic table and began gathering up paper plates. "You girls be careful," she warned Maggie and Blair. "I don't like the looks of them clouds over to the northwest. We're afixin' to get us some weather. The only question is what? Rain, hail, tornado, somethin'. I wouldn't go far, was I you."

"We won't." Maggie's gaze followed her grandmother's toward a brilliant blue sky decorated by a distant bank of fluffy gray-bellied clouds. "We'll ride along Horsethief Creek for a little way, then come right back. We'll be careful, I promise." She added to Chase, "If that's all right with you, of course."

"Of course." What else could he say, with his daughter glaring at him, just daring him to deprive her of this adventure?

MAGGIE, SITTING EASILY in the saddle, nodded toward a tangle of cottonwoods on the bank of the little creek. "That used to be my favorite hideout," she told Blair. "I made a little clearing, where I'd go to get away from my sister and brothers."

Blair grinned. She'd managed her horse quite well on the short ride, and her cockiness was evident in the way she copied Maggie's every move, including crossing her hands casually over the saddle horn.

"I never had any brothers or sisters," she said cheerfully. "Never will, either."

"Oh, now, you can't be sure of that." Maggie swung down and reached for the reins of Blair's horse while the girl dismounted. "One or both of your parents might—"

"No chance!" Blair snorted scornfully. "Neither one of them likes children."

"They like you." Maggie dropped the reins, effectively ground-tying their mounts, then led the way to a handy tree trunk where she sat down.

"No, they don't. They're *stuck* with me."

"I can't believe that."

"It's true."

Suddenly the girl wasn't joking; she was dead serious. Tears welled in hazel eyes very like her father's. For an unguarded instant, Maggie wondered what Blair's mother was like. What kind of woman had playboy Chase Britton wanted enough to marry?

"Blair, I'm sure—"

"I thought you were on *my* side, Maggie," Blair interrupted in a little-girl voice.

"I am, but—"

"You don't like him, either. You admitted it."

Maggie shifted on her uncomfortable seat. "That's not exactly what I said. I said—with a little help from you—we had no chemistry. That's not the same thing."

Blair shrugged. "It is to me. Daddy's such a jerk. He didn't even come to *see* me for years. Now all of a sudden he makes me live with him and he's telling me what I can and can't do—mostly can't."

Maggie clenched her hands in her lap to resist the urge to put her arms around this bewildered child. "Honey, don't you think you ought to give him a chance?"

To her surprise, Blair nodded. "I'm going to give him a chance, all right. I've decided what it is I really want, just like you said I should."

"Like I . . . ?" Maggie caught her breath, trying to recall what she'd said during their brief conversation in the ladies' lounge in Aspen. Something about catching more flies with honey. "Maybe you'd better explain that."

"It's obvious." Blair thrust out her lower lip in an increasingly familiar gesture. "What I want most of all is for you to please, *please* come be my tutor this summer. Joey told me you were the best teacher in the whole world. I . . . I need you." She hung her head as if ashamed.

Maggie felt sick to her stomach. She considered herself a tough customer, well able to withstand her family's none-too-subtle conspiracies to get her back into the mainstream after her husband's death. Nor did Chase present much of a problem; he hadn't offered her the job and she doubted he would, even if she were the last teacher left in the state of Colorado—which of course she wasn't.

But to resist the appeals of a child, this child, a needy little girl . . . Maggie swallowed hard.

Blair looked up quickly. "Don't you understand?" she asked plaintively. "You're probably the only teacher in the world who wouldn't fall all over him." She curled her lip. "I don't know what they see in him, anyway."

"They, who?"

"Women!"

"How many has he interviewed for this job?" Maggie asked faintly.

"Too many, but that's not what I mean. I'm talking about a whole parade of women through the house, falling all over him." Blair made a face. "It's disgusting."

Maggie stared at the girl, appalled. Was Chase the kind of man who'd subject his impressionable daughter to such shenanigans?

Blair sighed forlornly. "If you were there, I don't think they'd have the nerve to hang around, do you? I mean, nobody cares what *I* think. *I'm* just a kid. But you're a grown-up. You could give them that *look* and scare them away."

"What look?"

"You know, the one you're always giving Daddy. But there's something else that makes you my last hope."

Maggie's head was spinning. "And that is?"

"He'd never wrap *you* around his little finger. You're the only—"

The leaves rattled above their head, startling them both. At first Maggie couldn't figure out what it was, then realized that icy pellets of hail were falling.

She glanced at the sky, then grabbed Blair's hand and squeezed it urgently. "We've got to get back before it really opens up," she said. "I'm going to put you on your horse and I want you to grab the saddle horn with both hands and hang on tight. Can you do that for me?"

Blair looked excited, not scared. "Sure," she agreed readily, "but how will I steer if I'm hanging on?"

Maggie laughed and started toward the horses. "You won't have to, because I'll be leading your horse. We've got to move out, and I don't want to risk leaving you behind or having to chase you down if your horse decides to take off for parts unknown."

She gave Blair a boost into the saddle. "You okay with this?"

Blair nodded eagerly. "Are we going to *run?*"

"Like the wind!" Maggie swung up on her own mount and reached for Blair's reins. Hail pelted down, but it was still the slightly slushy variety, cold but not painful when it hit. "Ready?"

"Ready!" Blair's face glowed with excitement.

"Then say your prayers and hang on tight!" Wrapping the extra set of reins around the saddle horn, Maggie kicked her heels into her horse's ribs.

HE SHOULDN'T HAVE let her go. Grim-faced with worry, Chase reached for a saddle hanging against a wall of the barn. Nobody else seemed worried but they didn't understand; Blair was just a kid, and she hadn't grown up in these crazy mountains the way the Camerons had. She was from California; she'd panic. For all he knew, Maggie would panic.

Two horses raced into the barn through the big open double doors. Chase jumped back, barely avoiding flying hooves. He had just a glimpse of the riders before the animals skidded to a stop.

Maggie stepped down, her movements easy and graceful. Her words were anything but. "What are you trying to do, get yourself killed?"

Chase felt his jaw clench, but he kept his tone even. "I was *trying* to saddle a horse to come look for my daughter." He stepped toward Blair. "Are you all right, sweetheart? You scared me."

From her perch in the saddle, Blair looked at him with barely concealed disdain. "What do you think I am, a baby? Of course I'm all right." She threw her right leg over the cantle, kicked her left foot free of the stirrup and slid down as if she'd been doing it all her life.

"But you're soaking wet." He stated the obvious.

Maggie grimaced. "You think she'll melt? We're both soaking wet."

"It's railing," Blair said.

"It's what?"

"Railing—part rain, part hail. Sometimes it snails—part snow, part hail. Right, Maggie?"

"That's what we call it at the Straight Arrow." Maggie hooked a stirrup over the saddle horn and reached for the cinch.

"Let me do that." Chase put his hands on Maggie's shoulders, intending to move her aside. The wet fabric of her shirt was cold, the flesh beneath surprisingly warm and firm.

She resisted. "I can unsaddle my own broncs, thank you very much." She jerked away and his hands fell to his sides.

"Have it your way." If his jaw got much tighter, it'd lock up on him. "I'll take care of Blair's horse then." He turned to his daughter. "Sweetheart, you go on to the house and warm up, okay?"

She opened her mouth as if to give him an argument, then glanced at Maggie and shrugged. "Okay, Maggie?"

"Sure." Maggie dragged the heavy stock saddle from the horse's back.

"Don't forget what we talked about." This time Blair's glance darted toward her father.

"As if I could," Maggie said grimly. "You get on out of here. Tell Julie I said to find you something dry to wear—one of my sweatshirts, maybe."

"Okay." Blair dashed through the doorway and into the yard, where the sun now shone cheerfully.

Maggie hefted the saddle onto a handy sawhorse and turned toward Chase. "I'm sorry we worried you. We—" She stopped speaking abruptly.

Because Chase was looking at her in a way she hadn't been looked at in a long, long time....

3

SUDDENLY AND HORRIBLY self-conscious before his frank
appraisal, she glanced down quickly at the wet shirt
plastered to her skin from shoulder to waist. The out-
line of her bra showed clearly, as did the swell of generous breasts. With his gaze steadfastly upon her, she
felt her nipples tighten into hard peaks, and there wasn't
a damn thing she could do about it.

Except retreat to the opposite side of her horse, which
she quickly did. She shivered. His gaze had affected her
almost like a touch. She reached for the bridle, furious
at the way her hands trembled.

He cleared his throat. "Yeah, well...uh, I guess I
overreacted, but I'm not very experienced at this parent stuff."

"No kidding." She slipped the bridle off and wrapped
one arm around the horse's neck. "Anything else?"

"Yeah, now that you mention it. What did Blair want
you to remember?"

Maggie considered. Unfortunately she couldn't avoid
looking at Chase while she did it, which reminded her
of the things Blair had said about him. She could certainly see why women pursued him. He was rich,
handsome and sexy as all get out.

He was also a dude—tan slacks and yellow knit shirt, expensive leather sneakers, instead of boots. Not a wimp, though. His arms were muscular, his shoulders broad and his waist narrow. Somehow she thought he'd give a good account of himself in a brawl.

He could not, however, be trusted. He was the type to take advantage of any situation, especially where women were concerned. She'd known that before hearing it from Blair, who'd done nothing more than offer confirmation. After living with her mother all her life, how did it happen that Blair had suddenly been sent to her father?

That father smiled and Maggie's knees went a little weak; she was glad she had a horse to hang on to.

"Come on," he coaxed, "tell me what you two talked about. Maybe it'll help me understand her. I try, but I haven't paid any attention to adolescent girls since I was an adolescent boy. Can't you help me, even a little?"

"Sure." Maggie tightened her hold on the horse. Chase seemed so sincere, so appealing, but he didn't fool her. "She told me you're a jerk and she begged me to tutor her this summer. I think what she really wants is a champion for her side."

Chase looked disgusted. "And your response?"

"I told her to forget it, that no way would you consider me for the job even if I wanted it, which I don't." She led the horse toward the opposite end of the barn where doors opened into a corral. She felt enormously pleased that she'd managed to answer him calmly and rationally.

He followed at her heels. "What about the rest of it, the part where she called me a jerk?"

Maggie released the horse into the corral and stepped back, giving the bay a smart slap on the rump. "I told her she should give you a chance," she said. "Now if you'll excuse me—"

"Hang on a minute."

"Oh, for heaven's—"

"I didn't know."

Realizing instantly he was telling her he hadn't known Chuck was an invalid, she felt the blood drain from her face. "Whether you knew or not is totally beside the point," she said through clenched teeth. "It simply doesn't matter."

"Yeah, it does, because it explains—"

"Nothing! It explains nothing!" Slipping between the poles of the corral, she was gone.

So WHAT CHOICE did he really have? Chase wondered as he returned to the house. Every time he opened his mouth, she liked him less; yet Blair wanted Maggie, and he wanted what was best for his daughter. She had to be willing to work with a tutor, or it wouldn't do any good to hire one, would it? But Maggie Colby, of all people!

Prickly outspoken Maggie. What would her presence in his house mean—besides putting a serious crimp in his social life? He flashed back on the surprising sight of her standing in the barn, her shirt plastered to her body. He'd seen the lush promise of her breasts beneath the wet fabric, more than an eyeful even before her nipples puckered into sharp points beneath his approving gaze. Now he knew at least a little about what she hid beneath baggy clothing and a chilly manner.

A damned waste—not that he cared. He'd never lay a hand on her—for a lot of reasons, Blair and Betsy being but two. He had yet to earn his daughter's respect, and he wanted to keep Betsy's.

Having Maggie in his house would mess up his love life, but what the hell? Women were a dime a dozen, but he only had one daughter. Considering all the trouble she'd been giving him, one was probably plenty.

So he waited for his chance, and with so many Camerons milling around, it was a while coming. When the opportunity arose, he sidled up to Maggie where she stood momentarily alone at the living-room window looking out on a verdant meadow at the foot of an evergreen-swathed mountain. She'd replaced her wet shirt with a sweatshirt that obscured her body beneath thick folds of fabric, and she'd rebraided her long dark hair. Chase wondered idly how she'd look if she ever let that heavy mane tumble free around her shoulders.

She gave him a wary glance. "Yes?"

"I've been thinking..." He stepped up beside her, close but not touching.

She shivered and took a quick step away. "About?"

"Blair. You. I'm astounded at the way you two have hit it off."

She shrugged. "I like kids."

"But Blair hardly likes anyone. She's made exactly one friend since she came to Colorado."

"She's a kid. Give her time." Maggie wrapped her arms around her waist and edged farther away. "If that's all you wanted to say, I think I'll go see if Granny needs—"

"It's not all." He'd never noticed before, but her brown eyes had golden flecks around the irises, and her lashes were long and curling. Quite beautiful, really. . . He pulled himself back to the business at hand. "Blair's right. You'd be the perfect tutor for her. I've decided to offer you the job—officially."

Not a flicker of reaction crossed her face. "Thanks but no thanks—officially." She turned her back on him, walked to the couch and sat down.

He'd have been disappointed if she'd reacted in any other way. Following her, he sat beside her on the green corduroy cushions. "I'm desperate. I'm also prepared to overpay you shamefully."

That almost earned him a smile. "Even so, it wouldn't make economic sense for me. I'd have to find a place in Aspen, where even a closet costs more than I could afford."

"Don't be ridiculous."

She darted him a skeptical glance. "I couldn't commute over Independence Pass every day, if that's what you're suggesting."

"Of course not. You'll stay with Blair and me. I'll give you a generous salary, plus room and board."

She recoiled. "No way!"

"Hey, I don't expect you to do floors and windows."
When she didn't respond to his attempt at charming
repartee, he resorted to sober sincerity. "Relax, Maggie. Your virtue is safe with me, if that's what you're
worried about. I've got staff living there, too—housekeeper, gardener. What I *don't* have is somebody with
my daughter's best interests at heart."

She shook her head. "No."

He frowned. "I don't get it. Betsy said you need the
money."

"Betsy's got a big mouth."

"And a big heart."

Maggie remained unyielding. "I don't want to spend
the summer with you, Chase Britton."

"Give me one good reason why not. I said *good* reason."

She gritted her teeth, started to speak, stopped. Finally she said, "Here's a good reason. I don't like you."

He opened his mouth to tell her he returned the sentiment—in spades! But then he realized he was going
to have to rethink that position in light of new information.

He was still casting about for a response when Blair
came into the room with Lisa Marie and Joey right behind her. She gave her father a narrow glance, took a
deep breath and marched up to the couch.

"Well?" she demanded, looking from one to the
other. "Are you going to be my tutor, Maggie?"

Maggie shook her head. "I'm sorry, I thought you
understood. It would never work out."

"Okay," Blair said in a tone that suggested she'd been prepared for such an eventuality. "On to Plan B."

"Plan B?" *Now what?* Chase wondered with resignation. The kid must lie awake nights dreaming up ways to bug him.

Blair nodded. "Plan B—Switzerland." She looked at Maggie. "I took your advice. If you won't tutor me, my second choice is boarding school in Switzerland." She crossed her arms over her chest, prepared for battle.

"Switzerland!" Chase had been blindsided this time. "Maggie said you should go to school in—?"

"I never did," Maggie denied.

"You must have told her something!"

"I told her, no, *suggested* she might be happier if she stopped being a brat and—"

"You never called me a brat! Is that what you really think of me? I thought you were my friend!"

"I *am* your friend, but sometimes you do act like—"

"Let's get back to Switzerland, shall we?" Chase said. "Blair, did Maggie ever utter the word 'Switzerland' in your presence?"

"No, I thought of it all by myself," Blair said with evident pride. "I have a friend whose big sister goes to school there. She thinks it's great. What Maggie said was I should think about what I really want."

"Instead of . . ." Maggie gestured with one hand, trying to pull the rest of it out of the girl.

"Instead of making myself look bad by trying to make *you* look bad," Blair muttered, refusing to meet her father's gaze. "So that's what I did. I thought about it, and if I can't have Maggie, Switzerland is the only answer."

"No." Chase's face was set and hard.

"But—"

"I won't discuss it. The answer is no."

"Then let me live with Mama!" Blair's rage spilled over; she trembled with it, and tears streaked her cheeks.

The muscles in Chase's stomach clenched to the point of pain. "That's impossible."

They were making a scene; all other conversation and movement in the room had ceased. Joey and Lisa Marie sidled away to stand by Betsy, but they watched with fascination on their young faces. They'd seen verbal fights before; they couldn't live in the middle of a clan this size without emotions spilling over from time to time.

But perhaps they'd never seen such raw emotion as that conveyed by Blair's youthful fury; certainly Maggie never had. The girl looked ready to throw herself at her father, kicking and clawing, but she also looked vulnerable enough to shatter into a thousand pieces if anyone touched her.

And Chase...Chase seemed helpless before his child's enmity. Sympathy for him rose in Maggie, surprising her, frightening her. She pushed it down ruthlessly.

Blair wasn't finished with him by a long shot. "This is all your fault," she accused. "You made Mama give me up. I don't know how, but I hate you for it. I guess you wanted to get even with her for . . . for something, and you always get your way."

"Blair." Chase's voice was thick. "You don't understand."

She lifted her chin, disregarding her tears as if denial would make them invisible. "Then explain it to me. Explain why you ignored me all those years, and why you made Mama's life miserable. I'd like to know. I really would."

It wasn't the first time Maggie had seen Blair challenge her father, nor was it the first time she'd seen him back down.

"What happened...between your mother and me has nothing to do with how we feel about you," Chase said. "I won't let you go to Switzerland because I want you with me, not a million miles away ten months out of the year."

"Why?" It was a cry of anguish.

"You're my daughter."

"So what?" She shook her head in violent denial. "It's because you're mean and cheap, just like—" All of a sudden, Blair seemed to realize she was the focus of every eye in the room. Her face paled and she took a step back. "I'm sorry," she whispered, looking everywhere except at her father. "I hope I didn't—"

Whirling, she took a few stiff steps and stopped, as if she had no idea where she might go now, what she might do to regain her composure.

Julie, who'd just bidden her fiancé a lingering farewell, had returned in time to catch the fireworks. She put a friendly arm around the girl's trembling shoulders. "Let's you and me go outside for a breath of fresh air," she suggested as if nothing at all had happened. "We've got a new colt I bet you'd like to see. He's a beauty. Black with a blaze and two white feet..." Speaking softly, she led Blair out of the house.

"Oh, dear," Betsy said helplessly, "I never imagined..."

Chase sucked in a ragged breath. "My apologies to all of you."

"Oh, pshaw!" Granny whipped her dish towel against her leg. "These things happen. Don't worry about us. Just you get to work figurin' out a way to help that child. She's hurtin'." Granny disappeared back inside her kitchen, taking Lisa Marie and Joey, both still wide-eyed, with her.

Chase turned to Maggie. "You haven't said anything yet," he invited warily.

"What's there to say?" She was upset by what had just happened, and showed it. "Except... I didn't suggest she go away to school, really I didn't." She couldn't meet his eyes. "I should've kept my big mouth shut. I apologize for sticking my nose into your business."

"You could make it up by working with her this summer," Chase said. "Don't you see how much she needs you?"

Her head snapped back around. "That's blackmail," she accused.

"Only if it works."

"It won't."

"Then it's just another failed attempt to help my daughter." He dragged his knuckles over the ridged fabric covering the couch. "Would you mind telling me why you're so adamant about this? It's only for a few months, and I'll pay you at least twice what you could make anywhere else. You'll have every luxury and a free hand with Blair. Your word will be law where she's concerned. Hell, you couldn't possibly do a worse job than I have."

She didn't respond to his self-deprecating remark, just met his beseeching gaze with her own hard one.

He sighed. "Okay, so it's strictly personal. I know when I'm licked. I'll keep looking. Surely there's someone else out there who can get through to her."

He'd better find that someone *fast*, Maggie thought, forcing herself to remain aloof when, minutes later, he collected his now subdued daughter and ushered her into his car. Watching them drive away, Maggie tried to convince herself they weren't her problem. Neither father nor daughter had a right to drag her into their unhappy lives. She'd done the right thing, the only thing.

So why did she feel so awful?

When her family got through with her, she felt even worse.

Betsy, being more gently reared than her husband and in-laws, just pursed her lips and shook her head as if in painful disappointment.

But Ben jumped right in. "I don't like Chase Britton any better than you do—" a glance in his wife's direction clearly spelled out the reasons "—but nobody's askin' you to sleep with the guy, Maggie. Just teach his kid enough to make it to seventh grade next fall and charge him a mint to do it." His tone softened. "She's not a bad kid, even if she does have a smart mouth on her. She sure could use some TLC, though."

Betsy stared at her husband in openmouthed amazement, then threw her arms around his neck. She was no more surprised than Maggie to realize Ben had actually said something halfway sensitive.

It had taken Maggie a moment to catch on to that part, because she'd gotten hung up on the first part: *nobody's askin' you to sleep with the guy....*

What if somebody did? What if *he* did, Chase Britton himself, in a moment of ... insanity? It was ridiculous to think about it, but she did. She'd been celibate for more than a dozen years, and not by choice, either. With a husband paralyzed from the waist down, she thought she'd come to terms with the kind of sexual frustration that had her writhing on cool sheets warming beneath the friction of her hungry body or galloping through the night on a fast horse.

While she was being faithful to her wedding vows, the world had passed her by. Now a widow, she had no idea how to find her way back onto the field for the games men and women played. Being around Chase reinforced her insecurities. If she ever allowed him to puncture her composure—as she'd very nearly done the night they met—she'd be sunk.

Even so, she couldn't help remembering the way he'd looked at her in the barn, the way his gaze had lingered on her breasts beneath the wet fabric of her shirt. For one brief crazy moment she'd forgotten why she despised him so, lost in her desire to have him touch her—*more* than touch her. . . .

Julie joined the assault. "That kid's really messed up," she announced. "She blames Chase for everything from her mother's remarriage to the national debt."

"She doesn't know what a national debt is," Maggie protested.

"Mention it to her and she'll blame him. Honest, Maggie, Blair is a basket case. She really *really* needs you."

"She needs someone. It doesn't have to be me."

"Then think about the kid's father!" Julie sighed regretfully. "I wish I was a teacher, because I'd jump at the chance to play house with a great-looking guy like Chase Britton."

"For shame. You're an engaged woman."

"Well, you're not." Julie paused. "I feel for Chase. Poor guy doesn't deserve all this grief."

"How did you leap to that conclusion?"

"Why? Because . . ." Julie frowned. "You're not saying you believe Blair, are you?"

"I refuse to take sides."

"That's a new one. What happened to the old judgmental Maggie?"

That stung. "I've never been judgmental."

"In your dreams!" Julie looked suddenly uncomfortable. "On a more serious note, I have something for you." She held out a hand.

"What is it?" Maggie asked suspiciously.

"My savings account book. I've got $3,726.33 in the bank, and this time, you're taking it. I know it won't pay off what you owe, but it'll help."

Quick tears sprang to Maggie's eyes, and she blinked them away. "I've told you before, I can't take your savings, Julie. But I do appreciate the offer."

"Not to worry—I'm only twenty-five. There's time to save more."

Maggie managed a shaky smile. "And I'm only thirty-five. There's time for me to earn enough to pay off my debts. But I'll never forget you offered, little sister."

"Ben and Betsy offer, too. They said to tell you—"

"Don't say any more or I'm going to cry."

"You?" Julie scoffed. "The great stoic? Not a chance. Ben's set to sell off a few cows next week, and he figures that should bring in just about enough to pay the hospital and the doctors."

"It's also just about enough to fix the irrigation system in the north forty and buy that new bull he's been wanting." Maggie shook her head. "I appreciate it, but no, I can't allow any of you do this. You let me bring Chuck here after the accident, you put up with us for all those years . . . It's time for me to stand on my own."

She hugged Julie, speaking into the soft black hair. "But I'll never forget you offered, honey. Now run along before I *really* ruin my image."

MAGGIE SAT at the kitchen table with a cup of tea, a pad and a pencil, trying to figure some way out of her financial predicament. No solution presented itself, no matter how many hours she worked at the café. Wearily she propped her elbow on the table and leaned her cheek on her fist.

"Is it that bad?"

Maggie looked up with a smile for her grandmother. If the Straight Arrow Ranch had an anchor, it was Etta May Cameron. Maggie loved her grandmother dearly, but she wasn't sure she could take any more pressure today.

Grandma walked to the stove and picked up the teakettle. "Mind if I join you?"

"Of course not—unless you're planning to jump on me about taking that job like everybody else has been doing."

Etta May laughed. "Not me. I figure you're a big grown-up girl and you can make your own decisions. 'Course, like everybody else, I was findin' it hard to figure out what your problem is there for a while."

"Really?" Maggie arched her brows. "And what did you decide?"

"Well, it ain't the girl." Granny plunked a tea bag into her cup and carried it to the table. "You like her and she likes you."

No use denying that. Maggie nodded.

"And it ain't the money. I expect what he'd pay would be downright embarrassing to anybody used to workin' for a livin'."

"In all likelihood."

"That leaves the man."

Maggie let out her breath on a long sigh. "He's not our kind of people, that's for sure. He's rich and spoiled and used to getting his own way. I just don't like him, Granny. I'm glad you understand."

Granny frowned. "I understand, all right, but that's not *what.* You don't like him? Shoot, Maggie, I thought you liked him *too* much, or was scared you would. I thought you figured your reputation would be on the line if you moved into his house." Her laugh was self-deprecating. "Well, I'll be switched. I must be gettin' old. I sure missed the bull's-eye that time."

Maggie stared at her grandmother. Not that the old lady was a hundred percent wrong, but it wasn't Maggie's reputation she was worried about so much as . . . other things.

She would, however, accept the cop-out Granny offered. "Let's don't talk about the Brittons anymore, okay?"

"Fine and dandy. Let's talk about you."

Granny reached into her apron pocket and withdrew a tin box decorated with bright advertisements for a brand of crackers Maggie had never heard of. The old lady, gray eyes twinkling, set it in front of her granddaughter.

Maggie frowned. "What's this?"

"Little present from me to you."

"It's not my birthday."

"Good, 'cause it's not a birthday present. It's an I-love-you present. Go on, open it up."

Cautiously Maggie drew the box to her and swung open the hinged lid. Inside were stacks of money.

"A little better than five thousand dollars," Grandma said with satisfaction. "That's my butter-and-egg money. I been savin' for more'n fifty years." She shook her head, and wisps of dark hair, along with a few white strands, wafted around her face. "You'd think I'd have more to show for fifty years, but I have snuck out a few dollars from time to time. Just for emergencies, you see."

Numb with love and gratitude, Maggie stared at her grandmother, then back at the money. "Y-you always said your butter-and-egg money would buy you a fine funeral some day. I can't take this."

Granny grinned. "Take it. I've decided not to go."

"Oh, Grandma!" At last the tears came, the first since Chuck had been laid to rest. Maggie put her head down on her arms and sobbed.

After a few moments, Etta May laid a tender hand on Maggie's head. How many weeping Camerons had she comforted in her lifetime? "There, there," she said gently, "this, too, will pass. You're being tested, Maggie-girl. But every cloud has a silver lining, and you'll find yours one of these days. I guarantee it. In the meantime, you take this money and don't give it a second thought. Your welfare is worth more to me than all the money in the world."

Maggie lifted her head, drying the tears with her sleeve. "Thank you, Granny, but I won't take your money."

"Margaret Elnora Cameron!"

Maggie managed a shaky smile. "I won't take it because I won't need it. I—I'm going to call Chase Britton and tell him I've decided to accept the job."

Etta May's mouth curved into a pleased smile. "Well, my goodness, you've gone and changed your mind, after all." She leaned down to kiss her granddaughter on the temple. "I've a feelin' you won't regret it, honey-lamb."

"I only hope." Maggie closed her eyes, warmed by her grandmother's approval. But a silver lining still seemed very far away.

4

MAGGIE CALLED Chase that very night before she could lose her nerve. If she had to eat crow, then she would, but she would not take her grandmother's funeral money.

He answered on the fifth ring.

She took a deep breath. "This is Maggie Colby. If you're still interested, my answer is yes." *Damn, what a stupid way to put it!* When no immediate reply was forthcoming, she rushed on, "On the other hand, if you've already found a tutor for Blair, I quite understand." *Even stupider; he was at the ranch all day, not interviewing teachers.* Now what? She only had two feet to put in her mouth.

Or so she thought, until she heard a light feminine voice in the background. "Darling, you're going to miss the best part if you don't hurry!"

Maggie could have died of embarrassment. "Uh . . . I've caught you at a bad time . . ."

"Not at all."

It was as if he'd just that moment homed in on the conversation. Maybe he had; heaven only knew what she'd interrupted.

"I'll call back tomorrow," she lied.

"No!" A pause. "Do you mean it?"

"Yes, but don't feel you have to—"

"You're hired."

"—make any snap decis— I'm hired?"

"When can you start?"

"Wh-when do you want me?"

"Yesterday."

"Day after tomorrow?"

"Is that the best you can do?"

"T-tomorrow, then. But I won't be able to get there until late afternoon. I'll have to pack—" *am I really about to move in with some guy I don't even know?* "—and take care of a few things here first."

"Sounds fair."

"Where do I go?"

"Come to the restaurant. You can find it, can't you?"

"I think so."

"I'll be waiting for you."

She closed her eyes. The die was cast. "All right."

She hung up the phone and stood there for a few moments, trying to convince herself she was doing the right thing.

She was halfway up the stairs before she realized they hadn't even discussed salary.

UNLIKE HER BROTHER Ben, Maggie had always rather liked Aspen. Perhaps it was the scholar in her, but the checkered history of the village at the head of the Roaring Fork Valley had always seemed exotic and appealing.

Aspen was a Lady with a Past, which appealed to a lady with no past to speak of. The community had begun as a rough-and-ready mining town with fortunes in gold and silver wrenched from the earth, sometimes overnight.

After the silver crash of 1893, the little village slid into a decline that left it hardly more than a ghost town. In the mid-1930s, it was a forgotten community nestled eight thousand feet high in the central Rockies, flanked by six fourteen-thousand-foot peaks of the Elk Mountains—perfect, the world eventually realized, for winter sports. In the blink of an eye, the economy turned from silver to snow.

As she neared the town now, Maggie's pleasure in her surroundings faded before her trepidation. Yet by the time she'd come down off the pass and entered the outskirts of Aspen, she believed she'd come to grips with her situation.

This was a job, nothing more. It would not interfere with who and what she was: Maggie Colby, an independent woman with her feet firmly planted on the ground. She was not some featherheaded girl to be swept away by ritzy surroundings or charismatic companions, whatever—or whoever—they turned out to be.

This attitude, she felt confident, would fit right in with Chase Britton's plans. All he wanted was someone to help his daughter at this vulnerable juncture in her life. He thought Maggie was that person; so did she, or she wouldn't be here.

She pulled into the parking lot of his elegant restaurant on the mountainside. The view at night must be spectacular, she thought, crawling out of her '91 Chevy. Her ordinary blue car didn't look any too good among the sports cars and shiny all-terrain vehicles, but that didn't bother her. She'd never been impressed by wealth or its flashy symbols, and she wasn't about to change at this late date.

Inside, a hostess directed her down a long hallway. At his enormous black-and-silver door, she drew a deep breath and knocked sharply.

A deep voice invited her to enter. Maggie swallowed hard, opened the door and walked into Chase Britton's lair with her shoulders square and her jaw out.

WHEN HE SAW HER, Chase hid his sigh of relief. He'd half expected her to change her mind and not come at all. He'd half hoped she would.

He rose from his desk and crossed to meet her. "Glad you made it," he said cordially. "I'm sorry I rushed you, but I've got this fear that Blair's falling more behind each day." He shrugged and gave her a whimsical smile. "Time's awasting, and she's got a lot of academic ground to make up."

"I quite understand."

She offered her hand rather formally, and he took it in his for a brief greeting. Her fingers were icy, matching her personality, he thought.

She withdrew her hand and looked around with a frown. "Blair isn't here?"

"No. I haven't told her you're coming."

"Why not?"

"I didn't want to get her hopes up," Chase said frankly, "in case you didn't show." He waited for her reaction, curious to see if she'd take offense.

She just looked at him for a moment, her face smooth and impassive. Finally she said, "When I give my word, I keep it."

"That's good to know," he said. "I try to do the same. But although the spirit is willing, occasionally the flesh is weak." He indicated the door. "Shall we go to the house? It's not far, so perhaps you'd like to follow me in your car."

She nodded, adjusting the shoulder strap on her purse. He noticed that, as usual, she wore jeans and boots and a too-big yellow shirt with several turns in the long sleeves.

That disguise no longer fooled him. He held the office door for her, deliberately putting one hand on her waist to guide her toward his private exit. Beneath his palm he felt her flesh tighten, and she stepped aside so quickly it was almost a hop.

But her expression never changed. She was playing this cool, very cool.

That's fine with me, Chase assured himself, although in truth he couldn't remember the last time a woman had pulled away from his touch. But hell, if one was going to find him resistible, it might as well be Maggie Colby.

"Omigosh!"

Maggie forgot her recent vow to maintain her composure at all costs and stared, openmouthed, at Chase's house—it couldn't possibly be called a home. She'd expected something elaborate, even opulent, but she certainly hadn't expected *this:* a starkly geometric mansion perched all alone in a forest on the side of a mountain. It looked about as inviting as a high-tech prison.

They'd parked in an elaborate four-car garage concealed behind a mahogany door, all that was visible from the road. Chase, carrying her single suitcase, had led her through a back entryway and into a kind of courtyard with a wide stone pathway meandering to the house through a grove of aspen, fir and spruce.

He looked pleased by her spontaneous outburst. "Deegan Daws did it for me," he said with obvious satisfaction.

Was that name supposed to mean something to her? Chase obviously expected a response, but what could she say about something that looked to her like an expensive monstrosity? "It's . . . certainly different," she finally managed.

If he caught any touch of sarcasm, he didn't let on. "It is that," he agreed. "Come inside and meet Chloe."

Who was Chloe? Maggie wondered, following Chase along the path toward a doorway as bleakly forbidding to her eyes as everything else. But the path, she had to admit, was pretty. She drew in an appreciative breath of air redolent with the fragrance of evergreens. Birds darted between the trees, and occasionally one would call in raucous comment.

The entry opened into a white hallway as stark as the exterior of the house. Chase led her past several doors, then through one on the left that opened into the kitchen, all white and chrome, bright lighting and professional-looking appliances.

A woman leaned against a work island in the center, her frizzy red hair the first thing Maggie noticed—that and the fact that she was smoking a cigarette. Her skinny legs were encased in skintight red pants that ended midcalf. A black sequined sweater completed the ensemble.

She had to be sixty if she was a day.

Chase set the suitcase on the floor. "Chloe, I thought you promised not to smoke while Blair's in the house."

"Hell, Chase, she drove me to it." Chloe ground out her cigarette in a jar lid. She gave Maggie a plaintive glance. "That kid would try the patience of a saint."

"Which you're not," Chase tacked on. "Maggie, this is Chloe, my housekeeper. Chloe, Maggie, Blair's new teacher."

"Hallelujah!" Chloe said, her smile a scarlet slash.

Maggie felt immediate empathy for the woman, in spite of her unusual demeanor and dress. "Glad to meet you, Chloe."

"Not half as glad as I am," the woman declared bluntly. She straightened. "Can I go now, boss? Got a heavy date tonight." She hiked pencil-line eyebrows for emphasis.

"Yeah, run along. We'll see you tomorrow."

"Jeez, something else to look forward to." Grumbling under her breath, Chloe opened a drawer and pulled out a gold clutch purse. Extracting a mirror, she checked her makeup, applied fresh lipstick, thrust the purse beneath her arm, grinned and departed.

Chase and Maggie stood perfectly still until they heard the front door close. Then Maggie laughed in spite of herself. "Chloe must be one terrific housekeeper."

He groaned. "Not really, but what can I do? She's...an old friend of the family. Besides, I like her." Taking Maggie's arm, he steered her back into the hall. "Until Blair came, it wasn't much of a problem. But Chloe's not the best role model for an impressionable girl."

Maggie slid her elbow from his light grip, wanting to rub away the tingle but fearing that would be too obvious. "I can see that."

"You don't know the half of it. She's a former Vegas showgirl. I caught her teaching Blair to do a bump and grind yesterday."

He led Maggie into another room; could it be the living room? It was huge, all white and gray and silver. A freestanding round fireplace stood in the middle, surrounded by blocky modular couches and chairs. Four-foot-high mahogany built-ins provided a screen between this room and the dining area. Practically all wall space was taken up by windows, floor to ceiling.

And not a curtain or a blind anywhere. Maggie had never seen anything so stark and uninviting in her entire life. How could anyone live here, without a touch of color, not even a bright throw pillow or rug in sight?

Blair's voice preceded her into the room. "Chloe? Libby and I want a snack! We got any more potato chips, or did you eat them all?"

Maggie turned just as Blair sailed through the door, accompanied by another girl, one a little taller and perhaps a little older. Blair saw Maggie and stopped short, her eyes going wide.

Maggie smiled. "Surprise!" she said softly. "He talked me into it."

Blair started forward, a look of joy suffusing her face. Maggie dropped her tote bag of books on the floor and opened her arms.

BLAIR'S ROOM was upstairs at the end of the hall, and Maggie was assigned the room across from it. The bedrooms were practically identical: queen-size beds, built-in closets and cabinets, and boxy mahogany desks with matching chairs. Blair's bedspread was white, Maggie's a silvery gray, and that was the only basic difference. Each bedroom had its own compact bathroom, also identical.

Blair had put her mark on her space, though. As befit her age, she'd strewn personal items everywhere. Clothing littered the floor, posters of the latest teen heartthrobs covered three walls, and her boom box boomed most of the time, Maggie soon realized.

Chase's room—suite, whatever—was downstairs. Maggie could only imagine what it looked like.

When Maggie, Blair and Chase reassembled in the kitchen a few hours later for dinner, Chase rubbed his hands together with enthusiasm. "So what'll it be?" he asked Maggie cheerfully.

Did he expect her to cook? "I'm not bad with eggs," she said grudgingly, exaggerating only a little. "What have you got in the refrigerator? Anything we could just pop in the microwave?"

He stared at her, a frown creating lines on his broad forehead. "Leftovers! But . . ." His brow cleared. "Hey, I'm not asking you to cook!"

"Surely Blair doesn't—"

"Not me!" Blair looked horrified. "He keeps trying to make me, but I won't."

Chase bowed with a flourish. "How do you suppose I know the food in my restaurant's great if I can't cook?" he teased. "I'm not a pro, but I'm not bad. When Chloe's out, I do the honors." He walked to the sink and washed his hands, the muscles of his arms rippling beneath the smooth brown skin. "I didn't bring you here to slave over a hot stove," he added with a challenging glance at Maggie.

She felt her cheeks grow warm but refused to acknowledge any discomfort. "I was perfectly willing to try, but cooking's not my best thing," she said calmly. "If you'll excuse me, I'll go ahead with my unpacking. Just call me when it's time to eat."

Chase felt a flash of disappointment. "You can un-pack later," he coaxed. "Stay and have a glass of wine while I show you my stuff." Picking a frying pan off the rack suspended above the stove, he flipped it in the air and caught it with a flourish: "Ta-da!"

He saw no softening in her, none at all.

"Wine makes me sleepy, and I don't need to see your stuff to know you've got it," she said a bit tartly.

"I'll go with you," Blair announced.

Chase found himself alone and wondering what had happened. Damn, that Maggie Colby was a hard woman.

Nevertheless, he prepared a magnificent fettuccine Alfredo with green salad and garlic bread. He figured he had something to prove here, and succeeded, judging from the expression on her face when she took the first bite.

"Good?" he prodded when she made no comment.

"You're an excellent cook."

Talk about damning with faint praise. "It's too cheesy," he guessed, his confidence punctured. Maybe he'd read her wrong. But this had always been a sure-fire never-fail dish.

"There's no such thing as too cheesy." She took an-other small bite, concentrating on her plate.

"Not *enough* cheese, then." Damn, he'd had that provolone in the refrigerator too long; it had lost its zing.

"Daddy, will you give it a rest? Your fettuccini's great, like always." Blair had a way of making a compliment sound a lot like a knock.

Feathers ruffled, Chase subsided. He wasn't in the habit of fishing for compliments and he didn't like it. But he couldn't help watching every bite they ate, and when Maggie left a forkful in her pasta bowl he took it as a personal affront. But did he say anything? No! They'd just accuse him of—

"Hey, what are you doing?" He frowned at Maggie, who'd begun clearing the dishes.

"You cooked. It's only fair I clean up."

She looked at him with a level impersonal gaze that made him want to squirm. Why did she get to him this way? Why did he *let* her?

"Not on your first night." He favored her with a smile he knew to be charming; her expression didn't change one iota. "I'll do it, or we—"

He'd meant to add, *or we can do it together*, but never got the chance.

"That's very kind of you," she said. "I would like to get everything organized tonight, so Blair and I can get right to work tomorrow. Thank you, and good night."

She walked out, leaving him standing in the kitchen with figurative egg on his face. He turned to Blair with a scowl. "Okay, babe, it's you and me. You load the dishwasher while I put away the—"

"Sorry, Pop." She jumped off her stool, looking anything but sorry. "Maggie's already given me homework. I've got to get started."

"Homework! What do you think I am, stupid? How could she possibly have given you—"

"Reading," Blair said smugly. "I've got to read *Romeo and Juliet,* and the sooner I get started the better."

"Shakespeare? You've got to be kidding."

Blair laughed. "That's what *I* said when she told me. But you know what? She's serious, so I guess I better be, too. See you tomorrow."

With a wave, she departed. Chase looked around at the mess, irritated beyond measure. This wasn't how it was supposed to turn out.

He'd intended to cook a delightful dinner while Maggie and Blair kept him admiring company; next they'd eat to the tune of their praise for his culinary abilities; then together they'd clean up the kitchen before retiring to the pool for a moonlit swim.

Not that he planned to make any moves on Maggie, heaven forbid. But if they were all going to live in the same house, they might as well be on friendly terms.

So much for good intentions. Ms. Maggie Iceberg Colby hadn't even *started* to thaw.

To hell with it. He reached for the telephone.

IT TOOK MAGGIE exactly two days of observation to realize that life in the Britton abode was a three-ring circus without a ringmaster. To provide a decent learning environment for Blair, it would be necessary to cut out distractions and standardize the household routine without further delay.

It wasn't too difficult for her to piece together the current household schedule. Chloe usually wandered in from her quarters behind the kitchen at about nine, made a pot of coffee and sat down to smoke two or three cigarettes while she tried to think what she should do next. Chase, who came home late from the restaurant most nights, got up between ten and eleven and wandered around bleary-eyed for an hour or so before really waking up. There were constant telephone calls from women, all of them looking for him, sometimes one coming to the house to parade about in a short tight skirt and high skinny heels.

And then there was Blair herself. Maggie wasn't at all sure what sort of hours she was keeping. Some nights she ate at her father's restaurant, then spent the rest of the evening in his office, often falling asleep on the couch. Some evenings Chloe baby-sat—or perhaps it was the other way around; Chloe was such a ditz that Maggie wasn't sure who looked after whom. Some nights Blair stayed with her friend, Libby, whose family, including a seventeen-year-old brother, Jordan, lived a couple of miles down the mountain.

One of Maggie's first decisions was to bring all this nonsense to a screeching halt. For two days she watched the goings-on with tight lips and asked few questions. But on her third morning in Aspen, she arose at six, showered and dressed, then called Blair to breakfast by seven.

"You gotta be kidding," the girl muttered, stumbling into the kitchen and sitting on a stool at the counter. "I didn't get to bed until two."

"Only because you were listening to music." Maggie offered Blair a glass of orange juice.

"I was reading," Blair protested. She took a sip of juice and made a face. "I can listen to music and read at the same time." Her expression turned sly. "As a matter of fact, I was reading Shakespeare."

"Really? Then tell me, how old are Romeo and Juliet?"

"I don't know." Blair screwed up her face. "Twenty-one? Yeah, about twenty-one."

"Back to the drawing board, and this time *without* the music."

"But I can't think when it's too quiet."

"That's why I'm here—to teach you how to think in all circumstances. We'll start by—"

"What in hell is going on at this ungodly hour?"

At the sound of Chase's voice, Maggie spun around. She hadn't thought they'd disturb him, since his suite was fairly isolated from the rest of the house. Yet here he stood, just inside the doorway, hair tousled and one hand rising to stifle a huge yawn.

He wore nothing but a pair of navy blue shorts. Period. No shoes, no shirt. His muscular chest was smooth and gleaming, his thighs corded with muscle. Looking at him like that, nearly naked, roused reluctantly from his bed with warm sleep still upon him,

Maggie felt her heart give an uncertain little lurch. He looked so damned good . . .

She spoke brusquely. "Did we wake you? Sorry. We're just having breakfast. Would you care to join us?"

He sighed and shoved the disheveled hair away from his temples. The shorts fit snugly across a washboard-flat belly, leaving his navel exposed. Maggie regretted noticing.

"Where's Chloe?" He glanced around. "What time is it?"

"About a quarter past seven, which probably tips you off that Chloe hasn't shown up yet."

"Ha-ha, very funny." His eyes, still at half-mast, opened a fraction wider. "Is that coffee I smell?"

"Sit down and I'll pour you a cup."

He did, and she did. Blair watched him warily. "This was her idea, getting up in the middle of the night," she said, "so don't blame me."

The coffee was doing some good. "Okay," he agreed, "I won't." He looked at Maggie, who concentrated on her bowl of cold cereal. "What gives?"

She put down her spoon. "I'm attempting to bring order out of chaos. I'm going to try turning this into an environment conducive to learning."

"Say it in English," he suggested.

"Blair needs a stable home life if she is to reach her full potential. She needs more than just a tutor. She needs nourishing meals on a reliable schedule. She needs to go to bed and get up at the same time every day. She needs to spend quality time with her father and know that the people around her have their acts together."

"Chloe's an old friend. Not everybody succumbs to her charm, but I won't fire her on your say-so."

Maggie blinked in surprise. "I didn't suggest you should."

"And I'm not in a nine-to-five business. I can't—"

"I know that, Chase." She had to do a better job controlling her irritation. "But there *are* things that can be done and I intend to do them. Unless . . ."

"Unless what?"

He was fully awake now, alert to the conversation, looking at her as if he wasn't sure how she'd gotten in here.

She met his gaze levelly. "Unless you'd rather call the whole thing off. You did promise me a free hand."

Blair piped up with, "I can always go to school in Switzerland."

Chase rubbed a hand over his bristly jaw. "Switzerland wouldn't take you with your grades."

His negative attitude didn't faze Blair. "What if I work really really hard with Maggie this summer, make up all my grades? Then will you let me go?"

Chase gritted his teeth. "Forget Switzerland. You'll work really really hard this summer, anyway, if you know what's good for you."

"Says who?" Blair sprang to her feet.

"Says me." His voice dropped to a lower more forbidding tone. "This is not negotiable, Blair."

She leaned forward and planted her fists on the countertop, but her lips trembled. "Why are you so mean to me? Why can't I ever have anything I want?"

"You wanted Maggie for a tutor and you got her."

"Well, now I want to go home!"

"You *are* home."

"This will never be my home!" Blair straightened, her young face flushed. "Why can't I live with Mother? You don't really want me here. You're just doing this out of spite."

"I do want you here," he protested. "You're my daughter."

"Don't remind me! Oh, I hate you!" She threw the words in his face with frightful relish. "You can force me to stay, but you can't force me to like you. And you can't force me to learn!"

Whirling, she ran from the room, leaving two horrified adults behind her. For a few moments Maggie and Chase sat there in unhappy silence.

Maggie hated feeling such sympathy for him, but she couldn't help it. She might not like him, but she had to believe he loved his daughter and was doing his best for her.

So she murmured, "Don't put too much stock in that. She's angry, that's all. And don't worry about our lessons, either. She'll learn. She's such a bright girl she won't be able to avoid it."

He looked only half-convinced. "Then why'd she do so badly in school?"

"To punish you," Maggie said. "There's no way in the world she could've failed one subject, let alone three, without it being deliberate."

He sighed. "Damn," he said softly, "what am I going to do, Maggie? I'm sure a flop at this father stuff."

"There's only one thing to do—keep trying." Was this the time to ask about Blair's mother? Maggie couldn't help feeling she'd do a better job with the daughter if she knew how and why the mother had lost custody after so many years—lost it or given it up.

"I notice you aren't rushing to reassure me I've still got a shot at Father of the Year."

He said it so plaintively she had to smile. "Hey, anything's possible."

He smiled back at her. "You know, I think that's the first smile I've gotten out of you since you came to Aspen. Nice. You should try it more often."

His words and the sudden intimacy of the look he gave her wiped the smile right off her face. She had to keep her distance from this man, she reminded herself, the thought tinged with desperation. It would be awfully easy to fall victim to his charm, and no good could possibly come of that. They came from different worlds, and she must never forget it.

But he was leaning across the counter, his beautiful hazel eyes warm and sincere. She didn't like being reminded how long his lashes were, how smooth and supple his skin. A strange lethargy crept over her, and she found herself staring at him, mesmerized.

He touched her cheek with his fingertips. "I know you didn't want to come, but you must know how much I appreciate what you're doing. You've already made a difference."

She should pull away. "I-if I have—"

"Chase, where are you?"

Maggie jerked as if zapped by electricity and swung toward the door just as a woman entered the kitchen— a very beautiful blond woman, wearing silk and linen and looking like a million bucks.

5

THE NEWCOMER stopped short, her brows soaring. "I didn't know you had company." She glanced from Maggie to Chase—who looked appalled.

"Jeez, Jessica," he said. "When did you— How did you—"

"Key." She dangled it from her fingertips by its chain. "Don't you remember giving it to me when—"

"I never—"

"Please excuse me." Maggie edged away awkwardly. Women walking in as if they owned the place at seven-thirty in the morning was a bit much, any way you cut it, she thought.

"I don't mean to drive you away," the blonde drawled.

"You're not," Maggie denied crisply. "I'm hired help around here, and duty calls."

Chase watched her go, his mouth tight. Then he turned to Jessica. "Give me the key," he said.

"But, Chase, darling, I told you I was having one made."

"No, you *threatened* to have one made." He gestured with his fingers. "I thought you were kidding, but since you weren't, pass it over."

She pouted prettily. "Think how handy it would be, the next time you need something picked up or delivered—"

"Jessica—"

"Oh, all right." She dropped it into his palm, then glanced toward the door. "Is she a live-in or just a ship passing in the night?"

Somehow her careless attitude irritated the hell out of Chase, but he didn't intend to let on. "She's Blair's tutor," he said evenly. "You remember me talking about my daughter, Blair? She's living with me now."

"And so's her tutor. How handy."

"Don't be a bitch, Jess."

She laughed; she'd always been a good sport. "Okay, if you insist. Can I have a cup of coffee before you throw me out? Aren't you even a little bit glad to see me? I probably wouldn't have come to Aspen at all this summer if I'd known you were going to be all tied up with your... daughter."

Now was his chance to tell her that he wouldn't be tied up at all, that they could resume their usual easy intimate relationship. Instead, he found himself nodding. "Yeah, it's a shame, but this father business takes a lot of time...."

Damn, what was he doing?

CHASE JOINED Maggie and Blair at breakfast the next morning, and the morning after that and the morning after that. Maggie's surprise turned to shock and, finally, to resignation. Although it couldn't be easy for him to make such a radical adjustment in his habits, he accomplished it without comment or, apparently, regret.

Maggie had no right to complain, although she wanted to. The last thing she needed was to start each day across the breakfast bar from a sleep-rumpled, half-dressed man so casually sexy she had trouble even looking at him without salacious thoughts. Still, she somehow managed to keep her mouth shut.

Blair had a bit more trouble. At first she seemed puzzled, which eventually gave way to sullenness. Now, on the morning of the seventh day since Maggie had instituted her new regime, the girl seemed determined to be as unpleasant as possible.

Thus it came as no surprise when Blair greeted Chase's invitation to join him for lunch at the restaurant with a surly "No chance! Why would I want to go back to that stuffy old place?"

Chase's lips tightened fractionally. "There's always a possibility, however faint, that you might enjoy spending time with your old dad."

"Why would I?" Blair was being deliberately rude, and they all knew it. "It's boring there. I'd rather stay here and eat Chloe's tuna salad with Maggie."

Chase glanced at his daughter's tutor. "Perhaps Maggie would like to come, too," he suggested smoothly.

The invitation sounded anything but sincere. Maggie shook her head, the braid sliding between her shoulder blades. "No, thank you." She added a hasty, "But it's kind of you to ask."

"See?" Blair shot him a vindictive glance. "Nobody wants to go to your old restaurant."

A tide of color rose in Chase's face; his daughter had obviously hit a nerve. "It might interest you to know that there's standing room only at my old restaurant every night of the week," he said tightly. "My old restaurant also pays the bills around here, including the one for the tutor teaching you what you damn well should've learned at that expensive private school last semester."

Blair thrust out her lower lip. "You don't have to get so uptight about it."

"I'm not getting uptight. I just want you to know there are some things we don't joke about."

Maggie had never seen the charming Chase Britton come this close to losing his temper. Time to intervene. "Blair, you misunderstand. I adore your father's restaurant, and it's very thoughtful of him to include me in his invitation. It's just that I don't have the time to—"

"You don't like him or his restaurant any more than I do." Blair jumped to her feet. "That's why you won't go—and neither will I!" She started for the door.

"Blair!" Chase slapped his napkin on the table. "Come back here! We need to talk about this."

"No way! I don't have anything to say to *you!*" She ran from the room.

Chase turned anguished eyes on Maggie. "This isn't working. Did I make a mistake bringing you here?"

The question hurt. "I didn't want to come," she reminded him.

"I know, but I thought once you were here you'd...I don't know, work with me, instead of against me."

"I'm not working against you!"

Chase fingered the handle of his coffee cup, his thick lashes sweeping across high cheekbones. His bare chest expanded with the force of an explosive breath. "It feels like it."

"I don't care what it feels like," Maggie said angrily. "I'm not working against you. I'm doing the best I can for Blair."

"Your best apparently doesn't include her father."

"Of course it does. It's just that . . . I've tried to be honest with her."

"About what?" He sounded completely baffled.

"Well, our . . . Well, you and I aren't exactly friends. She's a bright girl, so of course she's noticed a certain, uh, chill between us." Maggie struggled to find the words. "I tried to explain that sometimes people lack . . . chemistry."

"Chemistry." He looked at her thoughtfully, his head tilted as he gave her words due consideration. "Our problem is chemistry, all right, but it sure as hell isn't a lack. This is not the time to start playing those games, Maggie."

"Games! I don't play—"

"Jeez, it wouldn't kill you to forgive and forget. It was years ago and—"

"I *have* forgotten, or would if you'd stop rubbing my nose in it!"

Their gazes locked, hers furious and his calculating. Finally he said in a silky soft voice, "I have to wonder..."

"What?" The word burst from her lips, and she hated herself for asking. She didn't want any revelations from him, especially any that might further personalize what had to remain a strictly professional association.

"Forget it." He shook his head and stood up, towering above her, dominating her in some inexplicable way. "Blair's the only one who's important now. She's going to be living with me until she's old enough to be on her own, whether she likes it or not. We're damned well going to have to come to some compromise."

"She's just a child, Chase." Maggie knew she sounded coaxing, but the way he stood over her was intimidating in the extreme. "This is just a phase—I hope. She'll be in and out of many more before she's grown."

"You're probably right, but we have to find a way to coexist in the meantime." He glanced down at his heavy gold wristwatch. "Look, I've got an early appointment, so I have to get moving. Maybe we can talk more about this later."

She watched him stride from the room, long bare legs tawny beneath the navy shorts. How much responsibility must she take for his problems with his daughter? Perhaps what Maggie thought was honesty had actually been kerosene tossed thoughtlessly on Blair's burning resentment.

Not a pretty thought for a woman who always took responsibility—and took it very seriously.

BLAIR WAS particularly subdued that morning during her lessons. She responded with sullen irritation to Maggie's attempts to draw her into English and history; by the time they arrived at mathematics and the study of triangles, there was no longer any use pretending.

Maggie put down her dry-erase marker and wiped off the white board on which she'd been demonstrating differences between equilateral, isosceles and scalene triangles. "This isn't working, Blair," she admitted. "Do you want to talk about what happened at breakfast?"

"No!" Blair stared down at her hands, resting on top of her desk; a compact classroom had been assembled in the sitting area of her bedroom. Contradicting her own declaration, she plunged ahead. "He likes making me miserable. Mother warned me..." She shot Maggie a guilty glance.

So that was it. "What did your mother warn you?" she probed gently.

Blair shrugged. "Nothing."

"Please don't lie to me. I've thought for a long time there were probably...hard feelings between your parents."

"It's *his* fault. When they got divorced, he was awful. He's got a ton of money, but he wouldn't give us any. His whole family's got money, and they're just as stingy as he is. After he divorced Mama, he never came to see me . . ." She ran out of breath and stopped, her face flushed and unhappy.

"How old were you when your parents divorced?"

"Old enough to know what happened!"

"And your mother used to talk about your father, I guess."

"Wouldn't you? She gave up everything for him, her career and everything. Then he just threw us out for no reason. She was the one who took care of me, without any help from him. She loves me!"

"Your father loves you, too."

"Ha!" Blair scoffed. "If he loved me, why didn't he come see me once in a while?"

"If he didn't love you, why are you here now?" Maggie countered.

"To get even with Mama." Blair bit her lip against some struggle going on inside her. Finally she burst out, "She told me not to tell anyone, but I know you'll understand. She said people always took his side against her, and they'd take his side against me, too. But you're different, Maggie—you can't stand him, either! I can trust you to be on *my* side." She gave a high-pitched little-girl giggle. "Besides, you make him nuts, and I love it!"

Maggie wanted to hang her head in shame at her inadvertent role in all this. So Blair really had chosen her tutor on the basis of who would bug Daddy most. Maggie, who prided herself on being able to cut through to reality, had been had by a twelve-year-old girl.

"Blair," she began, "you really don't understand—"

"I don't need any lectures!" the girl cried. "I've got eyes—I can see. You do everything you can to avoid him, and when that doesn't work, you get all cold and . . . and snotty. Don't tell me I don't understand, because I do!"

Yes, Maggie thought, *I'm the one who hasn't understood. Cold and snotty? Am I really doing that? Do as I say, not as I do? Damn!* That would never work on a girl as bright as this one. Instead of making things better, Maggie had made them worse. The question was, how did she set about healing the wounds she'd unwittingly inflicted on the relationship?

Maggie closed the math book with a bang. "So you think you know all about it, do you? 'There are more things in heaven and earth, Horatio, Than are dreamt of in your philosophy.'"

"Huh?"

"Shakespeare. It means you may be a smart kid, but you're still a kid. Relationships can be so intricate that even the people involved don't understand them, let alone bystanders with their own axes to grind."

"What are you talking about, Maggie?" Blair tossed her pencil on the pad of paper where she'd been doodling triangles. "Sometimes I don't understand you at all."

"You'll understand this. Go wash your face and comb your hair. We're joining your father for lunch."

"What!" Blair jumped up, outraged. "I thought you were on my—"

"I am on your side, but you're not necessarily the best judge of where your side is. Do as I say, and I'll let you invite Libby to join us—for dinner, too, if you like. We'll barbecue out by the pool and swim."

"That's better." Blair's tight shoulders relaxed, and she smiled. "I'll hurry."

"You do that." Maggie headed to her own room to change out of her sweats and into something a bit more presentable, wondering how she was going to straighten all this out. Not for an instant did she doubt it was her responsibility to show the girl the error of her thinking.

CHASE WAS DELIGHTED to see them. Although he had no idea what had brought on this miraculous change, he was more than ready to let bygones be bygones.

With a flourish, he seated them at the best table in the house, the one with a view of the landscaped fountains outside the glass wall. Although Blair seemed a little edgy, her friend, Libby, joined Maggie in keeping the conversational ball rolling.

Maggie. Chase knew he had her to thank for this unexpected pleasure. An even more unexpected pleasure was the woman herself. He'd never seen her wear anything except sweats or jeans, sneakers or boots, but today she'd put on a long cream-colored skirt of crinkly cotton, topped by a short-sleeved silk blouse the same chocolate brown as her eyes. Leather sandals protected her gracefully arched feet, and she wore an assortment of turquoise Indian jewelry on wrists and fingers.

She'd even applied a little makeup, he recognized with a connoisseur's eye, including a ruby-tinted lip gloss that made her full mouth gleam invitingly. Maggie Colby was a handsome woman, but unlike most women he knew, dressing up didn't seem to have given her confidence; more the opposite. Could she possibly doubt the allure of her firm supple body and strong-featured face?

Blair couldn't maintain her stoic silence for long, not with her best friend chattering away happily. Soon both girls were laughing and talking exactly as they should be. When they opted for dessert—cheesecake for Blair and chocolate mousse for Libby—Maggie settled for a cup of almond-flavored coffee.

A surprisingly comfortable silence fell over the table while the girls ate. Chase noticed Maggie watching them, a slight smile tilting one corner of her full mouth. A shame she'd never had children of her own. Surely she felt their lack.

Her husband's accident had obviously changed her life, perhaps even her personality. What additional burdens that must have placed on a vital young woman like Maggie.

Chuck Colby had been dead for more than a year. In that time, she should have found someone else. She was in her prime, a strong beautiful woman—

Beautiful? Damn! When had he started thinking of her as beautiful?

Blair put down her fork and smiled with exaggerated sweetness. "Mind if Libby and I go outside to look at the fountains?"

"Yes, please." Libby's smile was more sincere. "And I'd like to thank you for the lunch, Mr. Britton. It was wonderful. Thank you so much for inviting me."

Blair tensed. "It was Maggie who invited you," she reminded her friend petulantly.

"But Mr. Britton is our host," Maggie inserted smoothly. "I'd like to thank him, too." She looked at him with a faint smile on those suddenly luscious-looking lips. "It *was* wonderful, Chase."

Chase, still thinking lascivious thoughts about Maggie, barely managed a smile. "Anytime, ladies."

Blair glared at him impatiently. "Well, can we?" she demanded waspishly.

"Can you what?"

"Go outside! Honestly, Daddy, don't you ever listen to me?"

"Go." He nodded toward the door, thinking that if she didn't, he might strangle her. Why did he have a shrew for a daughter, instead of a nice well-mannered girl like Libby?

"Chase, do you mind if I ask you a question?"

He turned back to Maggie. "Be my guest."

"How old was Blair when you and your wife split up?"

He grimaced. "You mean, for good?"

She nodded.

"Blair was . . . nineteen months old."

Maggie sighed. "She says she remembers it."

"Impossible."

"Yes. I think her mother's . . . well, there's no nice way to say this. I think her mother's done a number on her." She chewed on her lip, looking distinctly uncomfortable. "Was it a nasty divorce?"

"On a scale of one to ten with ten being worst, I'd say it was about, oh, a fifteen."

"That's what I was afraid of." She toyed with her knife, turning it over with her long sensitive fingers. "This is none of my business, but in light of the job I'm trying to do, in light of the communication problems you two have . . ."

"Hell, go ahead and ask your question," he invited, disgusted with himself for being in such a mess with his own daughter. If only he'd listened to his father the first time he'd brought Nikki home, none of this would have happened. Since it had, Chase accepted the responsibility.

"Do you have legal custody of Blair now?"

That startled him. "Yes."

"After all those years she spent with her mother, how did you pull that off? I'm no legal expert, but I've seen enough to know that it takes a lot to uproot a twelve-year-old girl from the only parent she's ever lived with and give her to the other. If what Blair says is true—that she saw very little of you while she was growing up— that makes such a switch even more unlikely."

He hated getting into this with Maggie, considering the problems they already had. "What's your guess?" he countered.

She sucked in a deep breath, and her full breasts rose beneath their silk covering. "I think . . . that transferring custody wasn't your idea at all. I think that for reasons of her own, Blair's mother more or less dumped her on you."

"That's what you think, is it?"

She nodded, her expression earnest. "Blair says you just want to cause trouble for her mother. She says you don't love her, you never loved her, but you took her away from her mother out of spite. She blames you for everything, thinks her mother is pining away without her and you don't even care."

Chase pressed his fingers to throbbing temples. "She actually told you this?"

"Most of it. Some I figured out from bits and pieces." She hesitated. "You do love her, don't you?"

"You have no right to ask me that question." He saw her recoil from his harsh tone and went on quickly. "Blair doesn't know as much as she thinks she does. For example, she has no idea that Nikki left me for another guy. Not that it mattered—the marriage was long over. But she took Blair with her and that *did* matter."

"Surely you could've spent some time with your daughter."

"I *did*. But I was busy building my restaurant in California, that and having a good time. I was a lousy father, I admit it. But Nikki made it harder than hell for me to see my little girl. I'd make arrangements to visit, they wouldn't be there. I'd ask for Blair for holidays, Nikki always had an excuse."

He was looking at Maggie, but he was no longer seeing her; he was sinking into a past too painful to be dredged up lightly. "For a while I kept trying, but then I started letting my visits slide. Hell, what was the point? Blair hardly knew me, and what she knew, she hated."

"Not hate, Chase."

"It feels like hate when you're on the receiving end of it." He glanced through the windows at the two girls walking near the edge of the fountain. One of those girls was his own flesh and blood, but he knew her hardly better than his neighbor's child. His jaw tightened with frustration. "At least Nikki could never say I shirked my financial obligation."

"Sorry, she's already said it. Since we've come this far...do you mind telling me how you got custody?"

"Nikki called six, seven months ago and said she was getting married to a record-company executive who didn't like children. I gathered she'd been having trouble with Blair because she didn't like her future step-father any more than he liked her. Nikki said she'd had the full responsibility of raising Blair and now it was my turn."

"Not too unreasonable, given the circumstances."

Chase looked down at the table, forcing himself to a painful frankness. "No? She said she'd drop Blair off with the clear understanding that she could come back for her whenever she wanted, no questions asked. Or for $250,000, I could have legal custody. My choice."

He heard Maggie's soft gasp and looked up to find her staring at him wide-eyed. He nodded.

"That's right. Basically I bought my own daughter, and I've been trying to make it up to her ever since." His grin felt a little lopsided. "I don't want her to know, for obvious reasons."

Maggie leaned forward. "Thank you for telling me. I thought Blair had been brainwashed, and now I'm sure of it."

Chase's load of guilt felt somehow lighter. "Will I ever get through to her?" he wondered aloud.

"Yes . . . but I don't think it'll be easy."

An understatement, if he'd ever heard one.

CHLOE ATTENDED the poolside barbecue that night, but Chase didn't. Watching Blair and Libby flipping burgers, Maggie told herself she was sorry about his absence only because she'd have to wait another day to tell him her plan.

She'd mulled over her plan all day, and it was basically quite simple: she would start being nice to Chase, talk about him in admiring terms, to set a good example for his daughter. And since Blair was not nearly as sophisticated as she thought she was, Maggie figured she'd have to be pretty blatant about it to make the point.

At the same time, she remained convinced that honesty was the best policy in all things, a conviction enforced by Blair's radar for detecting lies. Maggie would have to figure out what Chase's admirable traits were, heaven help her, before she could talk about them. And therein lay the danger.

Chloe nudged Maggie's arm. "Hey, wake up and hand me the catsup, will you?"

Maggie blinked herself back to the present. The girls were swimming, and only Chloe was still eating. Maggie handed over the catsup, appalled to see Chloe dump it over the potato salad. "What are you *doing?*"

"I like catsup." To prove it, Chloe took a healthy bite. "Say, Maggie . . ."

"Yes?" Something about the woman's tone set off warning bells.

"What do you think Chase would do if I quit?"

"Probably fire *me!* Is there a problem? Have I offended you? I thought we'd been getting along pretty well."

"All but you making me go outside to smoke." Chloe glared through eyes as lushly lashed as Tammy Faye Bakker's. "But that's not it." She sighed extravagantly. "Now that he's got you to keep things together, Chase doesn't need me. Well, really, he never did need me much. I'm not too hot a housekeeper, but it was better than charity. 'Course, he hired me in the first place because I used to be real . . . close to his old man."

Maggie's jaw dropped. "His old— You mean his father?"

Chloe scowled. "We didn't take up with each other until after Mrs. Britton passed on, so what was the harm?" Her expression grew nostalgic. "Chase was just a kid back then, and we got real close."

"He thinks the sun rises and sets on you," Maggie said honestly. "If you quit, he's going to blame me sure as shooting."

"I'll tell him otherwise."

Maggie sighed. "You weren't talking like this before I showed up. He *will* think it's my fault."

"He won't when he sees *this!*"

Chloe thrust out her left hand. On the third finger glittered the biggest rock Maggie had ever seen. "Omigosh!" she gasped. "Is that a diamond?"

Chloe yanked her hand away. "Hell, yes, it's a diamond. Do I look like a zircon sorta gal?"

"Of course not, but— Here, let me have another look."

Feigning insult, Chloe let Maggie admire the ring. "He wants to run off to Vegas, but I've been putting him off," she confided. "Now that you're here, there's no need to wait."

"I hope you'll think this over." Maggie couldn't imagine living in this house without Chloe around. "You know I'll be leaving in September when Blair goes back to school."

Chloe frowned. "I thought you were kidding about that."

"I wasn't!"

"You've got time to change your mind."

"Not a chance." Maggie chewed on her lower lip for a moment. "Maybe after your honeymoon, you'll want to come back to work," she suggested hopefully.

"Maybe pigs'll fly, but I'm not holding my breath." Chloe gave Maggie a hard punch on the arm. "Baby, my guy's *loaded!* I'm sailing off into the sunset with the man of my dreams. Fifth time's a charm!"

For her sake, Maggie hoped so. She'd better tell Chase about this right away, before he heard it somewhere else and leapt to the wrong conclusions. As much as she dreaded it, she should probably wait up for him and get it over with tonight.

6

CHASE LET HIMSELF into the silent house, moving with care so as not to disturb the sleeping occupants. He'd had a hell of an evening and was glad to be home.

Even with the unsettled state of affairs here. He did feel better for having told Maggie about his marriage and subsequent divorce, though the truth didn't exactly paint him in heroic colors. He could only hope she understood how hard he was trying to make up to Blair for a few of his past . . . not wrongs, for he'd intended no harm. Mistakes.

But he was the adult and Blair was the child. He shouldn't have let her discourage him. He had to build a relationship with her regardless of her mother's manipulations.

A light burned low in the living room, and he hesitated in the doorway. Chloe often left on extra lights— forgot to turn them off, more likely—but he knew for a fact she wasn't here.

Maggie never left lights on. Could something be wrong? Shoes silent on the plush carpeting, he walked into the room.

Maggie lay curled in the corner of a couch. She'd fallen asleep reading, a heavy-looking tome open across her midriff. He walked to her side and stood looking down. In sleep, she seemed much younger than the mid-thirties he supposed her to be. Long curving lashes lay in a lacy pattern on her cheeks, and her lips parted slightly at the corners as if her dreams were sweet. Her light summer robe gapped open, revealing the white gown beneath—and considerable cleavage. Her bare feet peeked from beneath the ruffled hem, her slippers lined up neatly on the floor beside her.

At first he didn't know what it was about her that held him there, and then it hit him: her hair. Glossy dark masses spilled around her face and shoulders, over the end of the couch. It was as beautiful as he'd imagined it would be. Without thought, he put out a hand to stroke the shiny length.

She sighed, a sensuous sound low in her throat, almost a purr.

He tensed, fearing she'd awake and find him standing over her at her most vulnerable. Instead, she turned her head, burrowing her cheek, catlike, into his hand. He dropped to his knees and slid his hand into the silken mass of her hair, curving his fingers to the fine shape of her skull. Sighing, she lifted her face to his in unwitting invitation.

Chase Britton did the only thing an honorable man could do under the circumstances: he slipped his hands free and stood up, breathing hard. But he couldn't make himself leave her quite yet.

Instead, he hitched one toe around an upholstered stool and pulled it up beside her. When he sat down, he jammed his hands beneath his thighs to avoid further temptation.

He couldn't touch her while she lay sleeping and defenseless. Was it dishonorable simply to look at her under those same circumstances? He didn't know, for he'd become entangled in some kind of almost mystical lethargy.

He examined her slumbering face with growing wonder. Her skin glowed tawny gold in the subtle lighting. Shadows emphasized the high cheekbones and a nose both straight and strong. Her lips looked fuller and infinitely softer than he'd ever noticed before, her brows more finely arched. That incredible dark hair spilling around her added its own erotic mystery.

This most invulnerable of women was made vulnerable by sleep. She sighed and her lush lips parted slightly.

Chase bit back a groan. Why had he never appreciated her beauty? Undone by the sheer desirability of her, he leaned closer, breathing in her warm and womanly essence. His body clenched and his head reeled with the unexpectedness of what he was feeling, what he was thinking . . .

About Maggie Colby, of all women.

He should wake her, send her off to bed or simply go himself and leave her here unknowing, but somehow he couldn't bring himself to do so. Instead, he thought about how it would feel to curve his hand over her shoulder. Her white summer robe was thin enough that he'd be able to feel the skin beneath, but not sheer enough to satisfy him. He longed to slide his hand along the curve of her shoulder, knowing she would respond by arching toward him, as she had pressed her cheek into his hand.

Her skin would be soft and warm, supple beneath his palm. He would drag his fingertips along the line of her jaw while his thumb stroked the little indentation beneath her lip. . . .

He was barely breathing, his every sense keyed in to the unexpected power of sexual fantasy. He'd been a callow youth the last time he'd become so overwhelmed by mindless wanting. He could hardly believe what was happening to him now, both above and below the waist.

He must be out of his mind—but why not? Since his daughter's arrival in Aspen, he'd been too busy and too worried to properly see to his social life. That had to be the explanation, since he wasn't the kind of man who lacked feminine companionship. He could pick up the telephone right now, even after midnight, and call any one of a dozen women who'd be delighted to give him what he needed.

But not exactly what he wanted, truly wanted: Maggie Colby, hot and hungry in his arms. His daughter's tutor, a woman who didn't even like him.

He would wake her, nothing more. That was simple and straightforward enough. She'd see him, make some caustic remark and drive all the desire right out of him. It was better that way, getting them back on their old safe confrontational footing.

But first... He leaned closer, seeking flaws to cool his fevered imagination. It must be the lateness of the hour, her intimate attire, the vulnerability of sleep. Tomorrow he'd wonder what the hell he'd been thinking.

She turned her head so unexpectedly that he had no time to retreat. He simply froze with her lips mere inches from his. All he needed to do was lean forward the tiniest bit and she would yield, without his ever having to ask.

But then what? He'd never intended anything to happen between them, even though he'd realized from the first that anything was possible....

Chase had met Maggie almost four years ago. He'd decided on a whim to drop in on Betsy Ross, a friend of long standing who'd recently moved from California to the little mountain town of Cupid. She'd been delighted to see him, flinging herself into his arms. Over her shoulder, he'd gotten his first glimpse of the two women who were now Betsy's sisters-in-law.

Both seemed stunned by his unannounced arrival. They'd been in the very act of hustling Betsy out the door to go with them to the Hideout, the honky-tonk on the edge of town. Chase's arrival had thrown a monkey wrench into a conspiracy designed to bring Betsy and their brother, Ben, together.

When Betsy urged Chase to join them, he'd had no qualms about accepting. True, both sisters were cool, but within an hour, he had Julie eating out of his hand.

Maggie was another story entirely, sending out mixed messages in a big way. She found him sexually attractive; he couldn't possibly have been mistaken about that. When her shoulder brushed his, she jumped as if burned; when their glances met, hers grew hooded and somehow challenging. He caught her looking at his body, knew she was measuring his physical attributes as a potential lover might do.

He saw all this and thought he understood. She was attracted to him but didn't want to be. It was the man-woman thing; she could spend the evening glowering at him, but that was self-defense. She might not like Chase, the person, but she had the hots for Chase, the man.

He'd cataloged that information with ease. Then other matters claimed his attention; he was sur-rounded by women eager to dance with the new guy. Passed from partner to partner, he became a bit flus-tered until his sense of humor eventually reasserted it-self. Unfortunately this left him no time to spend with Betsy.

Then line-dancing was called.

He tried to beg off, but Maggie, who'd done her best to ignore him all evening, stood up abruptly. "Now that they've got you broken in, it's my turn," she an-nounced.

He was appalled. "Line-dancing? I don't think so."

Her brown eyes narrowed in a challenge he found curiously sexy. "Oh, come on," she said scornfully, "you danced with strangers. You mean to tell me you won't dance with the woman who brung ya?"

"You don't need a partner for line-dancing," Chase protested.

"I do," she shot back. "I'm shy."

Like hell. She was trying to keep him away from Betsy while Ben made his play. When Ben and Betsy walked out of the Hideout arm in arm a short time later, he suspected he'd been had—and good.

When he asked Maggie what was going on, she grinned. "Nature taking its course," she said smugly.

He owed her for that one. His chance came that same evening, when she realized she'd been stranded without a ride home. "I'll be glad to drive you," he offered innocently, but with malice aforethought.

"No way." With Betsy gone, she wasn't even pretending to be friendly. "I'll spend the night in town at Nancy's—that's Nancy Wyatt, Betsy's aunt."

Chase arched his brows. "You'd wake her at this hour?"

"I won't have to. I know where she hides the spare house key."

"Then I'll drive you there."

"It's just a few blocks. I can walk."

He followed her out of the bar. "It's dark. I can't let you—"

She swung around to face him on the steps, sparks of irritation shooting from her—defensive sparks he'd felt all evening. Covering up with a display of temper might make her feel better, but was no defense against a man as knowledgeable as he was. Maggie was a lot more interested in him than she cared to admit. He knew it.

"You have nothing to say about it," she snapped. "Look, I've tried to be polite, but it should be obvious even to you I don't want your company."

"You call that polite?"

"Compared to what I *wanted* to be, yes, that was damn polite. Don't make me blow it now."

"Maggie, Maggie." He shook his head regretfully, as if disappointed by such a weak defense. "I get the feeling no one can make you do anything."

"Including put up with you. You're Betsy's friend, not mine. You have no responsibility for me or my safety or my welfare. I can take care of myself."

She took off, walking fast. Just as fast, he followed. She gave him an angry glance in the moonlight.

"Why are you doing this?" she demanded. "Don't you know when you're not wanted?"

"Not really," he admitted, tempted to add that it happened to him so rarely he could hardly be blamed. "I can't let any female walk the streets alone at night. What if something happened to you?" She set a fast pace, and he had to hurry to keep up.

"This is Cupid, Mr. Britton, not California, not even Aspen. I'm perfectly safe."

"Save your breath, Ms. Cameron, and let me—"

She gasped and twisted in midstep, falling forward with a quick cry. Grabbing for any support, she found Chase, who caught her by the arms. Her momentum whipped her around and hard against his body. Suddenly he was holding her in the sort of intimate embrace neither had anticipated.

Her breasts pressed against his chest, her hips thrust against his. In a flash his entire body sprang to life. He saw her face, eyes wide with shock and mouth a silent O of protest, and knew she felt his erection against her stomach. To his surprise, she didn't pull away. He thought he heard a tiny gasp of . . . not protest, nothing like protest. More like . . . need.

Her hands closed around his biceps, her fingers biting into the muscle. "M-Mr. Britton . . . Chase . . . you don't understand. I'm not—"

"Me, neither," he said, and kissed her.

For an instant she remained totally still, her mouth cold and somehow shocked. But then her lips parted and she melted against him, her arms rising to glide around his neck, her hips moving against him. Almost as amazed as he was pleased by this turn of events, Chase slipped his tongue into her mouth. Running his hands down her sides, he leaned into her, cupping her bottom to lift her more intimately into the cradle of his hips and thighs.

He hadn't expected such hunger from this woman. The icy Maggie Cameron wasn't icy at all. How had she managed to fool a man as experienced as he?

When at last he lifted his head to catch a breath, she grabbed that respite to shove herself out of his embrace. Taking a shaky step backward, she dragged one hand across her mouth as if to scrub away his kiss.

Chase stared at her, completely perplexed. He hadn't forced himself upon her, of that he was absolutely certain. That kiss had been mutual.

"I tried to tell you." Her voice sounded raw.

"What? That you don't like guys? That you don't like me? That you don't like kissing? I don't believe you, sweetheart. You liked that very much indeed—and so did I. In fact—" he took a step, deliberately crowding her "—I suspect we'd be capable of making rather extraordinary music togeth—"

She banged a fist down on his chest. "Will you shut up and let me say this?" she cried. "I'm married! I'm not Maggie Cameron, I'm Maggie *Colby.*"

"Oh, hell!" Chase didn't mess with married women, not ever. As he liked to say, he had his standards; they were low, but they were his. "Why didn't you say so?"

"Do you expect me to believe you didn't know? Surely Betsy must have said someth—"

"Hold it right there." Rattled, Chase thrust his hands through his hair. "I do *not* come on to married women."

"Oh, sure. Then explain *this!*"

Their glances locked, sexual tension still so strong between them that Chase couldn't control his physical reactions. Nor could Maggie; she was trembling and wild-eyed.

He spoke softly, his voice the only part of him that wasn't hard as a miser's heart. "I'll explain it to you, but you won't like hearing it. Lady, you may have a husband, but he's not giving you what you need. If you think I was out of line, I apologize, and I swear to you that if I'd known you were married— Oh, to hell with it. Come on, I'll walk you wherever it is you're headed and we'll forget this ever happened."

"We're there." She pointed. "That's Nancy's house so you've done your duty. If we never meet again, Mr. Chase Britton, it'll be too soon. . . ."

He'd been inclined to agree, but he hadn't known then what he knew now. He'd thought Maggie a hypocrite of the worst sort, coming on to him until conscience got the better of her. Now he knew there'd been few kisses in her marriage and plenty of frustration— of every variety, but especially sexual.

Looking down at her sleeping form, he saw a faint film of perspiration had appeared on her forehead, despite the coolness of the room. What was she dreaming? What would her response be now, if he took her in his arms?

MAGGIE FLOATED free, weightless and soaring above all care and woe. The only time she'd felt this giddy, she'd been half-drunk on cheap champagne. But this was somehow different—and infinitely better.

With eyes still tightly closed, she struggled to remember where she was, to understand what was happening to her. Her cheeks felt hot, her entire body steamy and . . . ready. Dizzy with barely remembered sensations, she reached, her fingers touching a surface smooth and warm and—

"What—?" She sat up abruptly, the heavy book falling to the floor while her fingers lingered on Chase

Britton's cheek. Yanking her hand away, she pushed her hair back from her face, trying to remember.

He smiled, little laugh lines radiating from the corners of his clear hazel eyes. "Take it easy," he suggested mildly. "I didn't mean to wake you, but—" he shrugged "—I thought perhaps you fell asleep waiting up for me. Is anything wrong?"

"I . . ." She had to get hold of herself; she sucked in a deep breath. Blood tingled through her veins, heating her cheeks and rushing to settle heavily in places best left undisturbed. Some disquieting erotic dream hovered at the edges of her consciousness. A dream of *him?* "Oh," she said at last. "Yes, I did intend to wait up. I— I guess I fell asleep reading."

"I'm glad," he said, "because there's something I wanted to say to you, too."

Instantly suspicious, she leaned away from him, against the back of the couch. "What?"

"I wanted to thank you."

"Wh-what for?"

"Today. For getting Blair to come to lunch and behave in a civilized manner."

"You already thanked me for that." His smile sent little shivers through her. Could he possibly know how lethal it was?

The smile widened, deepening the dimples in each lean cheek. "I'm thanking you again. Blair's very important to me, Maggie, no matter what she believes."

"A-about that . . ." Maggie shifted on the couch, fearful of touching him. She felt awkward and exposed, half reclining in her nightgown with her un-bound hair falling around her face. What must he think of her? Once he'd thought she'd come on to him—and maybe she would have, if she'd been free, if she'd known how. Did he think she was doing it again? She lifted her head quickly, hoping to surprise some telling expression on his face.

She did, but not the one she expected. He was look-ing at her breasts, at the cleavage revealed by the gap-ing front of her robe and the drooping neckline of her gown. His expression made her want to close her eyes and groan. Instead, she tried again, "About that ... I think I may have been on the wrong track with Blair."

He lifted his gaze from her breasts, and she pulled her robe together.

He licked his lips and said, "Huh?"

"I suspected all along that Blair might have chosen me to tutor her because she knew I, er, knew we didn't much like each other."

His broad mouth tilted up at one corner. "Whatever makes you suggest such a thing?"

"Intuition," she said dryly. "As it turns out, I was right. She's playing us against each other, and we can't let her get away with it."

"I agree." He gave her an open look of appeal. "So what do we do?"

Maggie sighed. "I suppose I'll have to put forth an effort—a serious effort—to make your daughter aware of your ... your good points." It wasn't easy for her to say that.

"Think I've got any?" His eyes gleamed with a mocking humor at his own expense.

"You must. Betsy likes you," she conceded grimly. "I'll find your good points if it kills me."

He threw back his head and laughed. She stared at the strong column of his throat, her mouth dry. What was she doing to herself? "I didn't mean it that way," she said unhappily.

"I don't give a damn how you meant it. I'll be delighted to cooperate with *anything* that'll get me closer to my daughter."

"Then I guess we should . . . give it a go."

He caught her hands and lifted them to his mouth, pressing a kiss on the back of each. "Thanks, Maggie." His eyes gleamed with a frightening intimacy.

She yanked her hands away and put them in her lap, one covering the other in an attempt to stop the tingling of her skin. "Just don't get any ideas!" she snapped.

He didn't look at all offended. "What kind of ideas?"

"You know what kind. You accused me once of coming on to you . . ."

"Well, not exactly."

"Okay, you *thought* it. I just want to make it perfectly clear that if I'm nice to you, it's for Blair's sake, not mine, and certainly not yours."

"I see." His expression became solemn, although he didn't seem exactly deflated by her pronouncement.

"Be sure you do," she said righteously. "This is strictly in the line of duty and don't you forget it."

"Only if you let me."

"I won't." She gave her head a brisk nod. "There's something else. Chloe told me tonight that—"

"—she's quitting to get married."

"You know? How?"

"She came by to tell me herself—and say goodbye. She's gone."

"I hope she's not making a mistake."

"If she is, it won't be her first."

"Then you don't, you know, blame me?"

He frowned. "Why would I blame you?"

"I did come in here and sort of...make a few changes. You might have been justified if you thought I was too hard on her."

"Maggie, sweetheart." He looked as if he wanted to take her hands again, so she thrust them between her thighs to avoid such a possibility. "What do you think I am? Some kind of monster?"

"Not exactly, but—"

"I'm well aware you're a control freak—"

"I'm not!"

"—and ever eager to accept responsibility or blame, as the case may be—"

"No!"

"—and you made it crystal clear you didn't want to be here in the first place. But you misjudge me. I know *you*, but you don't know *me* at all."

"I do, and maybe better than you think," she suggested darkly.

"No way." He unwound long legs and rose from his stool. "How are you going to show my daughter that I'm a decent guy when you don't believe it yourself?"

"I didn't say I don't believe it," she objected uneasily. But she couldn't face him when she said it, and she sprang to her feet, embarrassed. "Look," she said desperately, "I've always believed that honesty is the best policy. If I'm going to sing your praises . . ."

"Sing my praises?"

"Blair's not into subtlety. If I'm going to sing your praises, I'll have to figure out what your praises are."

"Maybe I can help you," he said thoughtfully. "Good points . . . well, I've got a lot of money. Some of it I earned the old-fashioned way, but most of it's family loot."

She glared at him. "Money isn't everything."

"If you really believe that," he said dryly, "you're a traitor to your sex. *You* think of something."

"You're . . . reasonably good-looking."

"Thank you." He was all but laughing now. "Go on."

"You can be charming—even when you're also being a louse!" She gave him a phony smile and marched out of the room, his rich laughter following her.

Finding something to praise was actually frighteningly easy.

7

WHEN CHASE SAID he'd cooperate, he meant it. The next morning at breakfast he announced he'd be cutting back his hours at the restaurant, even taking some time off. What, he inquired of his daughter, would she like to do to make the summer special?

Maggie held her breath, hoping for the best.

She didn't get it.

"I'd like to spend it with Mama," Blair snapped back.

Chase didn't blink an eye. "What's your second choice?"

She glowered at him while poking viciously at her grapefruit. "Spend it at the Straight Arrow Ranch?"

A muscle jumped in Chase's jaw, but his pleasant expression never wavered. "What's your third choice?"

"Daddy! Why can't—"

"You could go to Denver," Maggie interjected, afraid to let Blair get too worked up. "There are lots of neat things to do there, museums and botanical gardens. And malls—I'm sure you enjoy shopping, don't you, Blair?"

Interest flickered in the girl's eyes, then died. "Denver's a hick town," she said. "Been there, done that."

Maggie's concerned gaze met Chase's above the girl's drooping head. For an instant, she thought she saw despair. She wasn't going to let Blair get away with this! "Have you ever gone swimming in a hot spring?" she asked.

"A what?"

"A hot spring, water that comes out of the ground already hot."

"Like at Yellowstone Park?"

Maggie nodded.

"Why would I want to swim in some stupid little hole in the ground?"

Maggie's mouth curved in a teasing smile. "Would you like to swim in the world's largest hot-springs *pool?*"

Blair looked intrigued in spite of herself. "The world's largest? I'll bet it's the size of a hot tub."

"Would you believe five hundred feet long?"

"You're putting me on," Blair said.

"I'm not."

"Sounds dumb."

"It's not," Maggie said. "It's fun. There's even a slide. And there are other things to do in Glenwood."

"Like what?"

"Like . . . like the grave of Doc Holliday."

"A grave!" Blair shuddered. "Wasn't Doc Holliday a TV cowboy or something?"

Chase rolled his eyes. "I can see you need a little instruction about the wild and woolly West. Doc Holliday was a famous gunfighting dentist, Wyatt Earp's pal. What do you say, shall we give it a go? Glenwood's only a little way from Aspen."

Blair's mouth turned down at the corners. She was going to say something rude and reject her father's proposal, Maggie thought. A glance at Chase told her he was prepared for the worst.

But Blair surprised everybody. "Okay" she agreed. "Why not? As long as Maggie comes along."

WHEN MAGGIE had mentioned the famous hot mineral pool an hour away from Aspen, she'd had no intention of becoming part of the package. Yet two days later she found herself in the Glenwood Springs bathhouse, changing into her swimsuit while Blair fidgeted.

The hot-springs lodge and pool lay near the juncture of the Colorado and Roaring Fork rivers, at the edge of the little resort town of Glenwood Springs. A permanent population of only six or seven thousand residents catered to tourists lured year-round by the hot springs, and in the winter by world-class skiing.

As Chase's Jaguar had carried the trio across the bridge over the Colorado River, Blair had looked down at the massive pool below them on the riverbank. The steam rising so copiously from the surface of the water swept away Blair's blasé pose.

"Wow!" she'd cried. "That's the biggest swimming pool I ever saw and it's hot!"

Maggie had felt the same astonishment the first time she'd seen it some twenty-five years ago. The *last* time she'd seen it . . . better not to dwell on that. Pulling a brightly flowered Hawaiian muumuu over her modest one-piece swimsuit, she grabbed a stack of towels and a beach bag before following Blair out onto the paved pool deck. Chase waited for them in the sunshine. Maggie took one look and nearly tripped.

What a sight he was in his red swim trunks, with his sinuous swimmer's physique: broad-shouldered, flat-bellied, sleek-muscled. Although not bulky, his was the body of a man, not a boy, and a superbly conditioned man at that. A white towel lay casually over one shoulder; mirrored glasses shielded his eyes.

He grinned and his teeth flashed a dazzling white. "Ready to jump in?" He tossed his towel over a lounge chair.

Maggie held back. "You two go ahead," she urged, still a little breathless from her first sight of him. "I think I'll stretch out in the sun for a few minutes."

"But..." He frowned and urged her toward him with one hand.

"Come on!" Blair said impatiently, starting toward the wide steps leading down into the enormous main pool. "Daddy! Let's go!"

"Go," Maggie said softly.

His questioning gaze held hers for just a moment before he turned away. She watched him grab his giggling daughter around the waist and drag her, screaming with delight, into the steamy water. Maggie had never seen them together like this, like a normal family. It was worth coming back to this place just for that, she told herself resolutely.

Lowering herself into a lounge chair, she closed her eyes, resting one forearm over them to be sure of blotting out her surroundings. This was a problem of her own making. She would deal with it.

CHASE SHOOK WATER from his hair like a wet retriever, then looked around for Maggie. He spotted her stretched out on a lounge in the shade.

She still wore that damned muumuu. When he'd first seen it, he'd almost burst into laughter. Now it was more a nuisance, for he was determined to see what lay beneath that missionary-prim exterior.

He had a pretty good idea. When he'd found her sleeping on his couch, he'd had a nice preview of full breasts and curving calves. In the intervening days, the more she covered up the more intrigued he became. Was she really that shy or was it just . . . him?

Winding his way through scattered chairs and sunbathers, he sat down on the edge of her lounge without warning. Her eyes flew open, and he saw shock and surprise, followed by a flash of welcome just before thick lashes swept down to provide concealment.

She tried to put a bit of distance between his hip pressing against her thigh, but the lounge was too narrow, and all her movement did was call attention to her uneasiness.

"Where's Blair?" she asked.

"She seems to have made a friend." He gestured with his chin to where Blair was splashing about with a girl her own age.

Maggie nodded. "It looks as if the two of you are getting along pretty well."

"Yes."

"I'm glad."

"Me, too. Thanks for suggesting this place."

"No problem."

"Except that you didn't want to come with us, and you especially didn't want to come here."

She wouldn't look at him. "Don't be ridiculous. I told you I'd be nice to you if it killed me."

"I get the feeling this almost did. What is it about Glenwood that gets to you, Maggie? The closer we got, the more anxious *you* got."

"You're mistaken." Her voice sounded flat and unconvincing.

"No, I'm not. Dammit, Maggie, don't you know what friends are for?"

"Friends?"

Her eyes flew wide, and he knew she'd never thought of him in that way. Adversary, yes; maybe even lover. But friend? He laughed. "I could be a friend if you'd let me. Tell me what you were thinking about when I walked up. You seemed a million miles away."

"No," she murmured. "I was a million *years* away." She licked her full lips. "The first time I came here was with my family. I was just a kid, and I thought it was the most fabulous place I'd ever seen." She smiled and pointed to the big old-fashioned gothic-looking sandstone lodge. "I thought for sure that building was haunted, which appealed to me greatly."

"You mean it isn't?" He spoke gently, for her voice trembled a little and he realized that all her memories of this place weren't so happy. "When was the last time you were here?" he asked with sudden inspiration.

"Chuck and I spent our honeymoon across the street there, at the Hotel Colorado," she said. "That was wonderful, too. When we left, we promised to come back every year on our anniversary."

She gazed out across the pool with its noisy swimmers and players, but he knew she wasn't seeing it. He remained silent, letting her take her time, trying to imagine what it must have been like for her and knowing he couldn't possibly.

After a moment she went on, "We couldn't keep our promise because—" she licked dry lips "—before our first anniversary, Chuck was in a wheelchair. I've never been back to Glenwood until today."

He wanted to take her in his arms and comfort her, pat her back and tell her everything would be all right. Maybe even kiss her—a gentle kiss of solace, nothing more. Before he could act on that impulse, she sat up abruptly.

"I don't know what's gotten into me, spilling my guts to you that way. Now that I'm here, I feel fine about it." Swinging her legs off the chair on the opposite side, she stood up. "I think I'll give the therapy pool a try. If you'll excuse me—"

"I'll join you," he said promptly, standing up. "I could use—"

"No!"

He stopped short, taken aback by her vehemence.

She looked apologetic. "I'm sorry. I don't mean to be rude, but you came here to spend time with Blair, and I think you should." She waved vaguely toward the large pool, then turned toward the small one where the mixture of hot-to-cold water allowed for considerably higher temperatures.

He hesitated, watching her walk quickly away. He wanted to go with her, but she wouldn't welcome his company.

That, he assured himself, would not always be the case. The self-contained Maggie Colby might fight it every step of the way, but she was slowly revealing her secrets. Satisfied, he turned away, searching among the bobbing heads and splashing bodies for his daughter.

"YOU HAD A ROTTEN TIME, Maggie. Admit it."

"I certainly did not!"

"You didn't even get in the big pool, just fooled around in that little one with all the *old* people."

"I . . . just didn't feel like swimming. Now will you please get ready for bed? You may not be tired, but I am."

Blair stuck to the subject that interested her. "You didn't feel like swimming because of *him*. You don't really like him, so why are you pretending?"

"I'm not." Maggie realized she wasn't going to be able to change the subject, and she sighed in resignation. "Listen, Blair, first impressions are sometimes wrong. Since I've been here I've gotten to know your father much better and—"

"That's such a lie!" Blair pulled her hands from Maggie's and backed away, her expression incredulous. "Is he paying you to say that?"

"Blair!"

"He paid you to come here and be my teacher. How should I know what you're willing to do for money?"

"I'm not willing to do anything that would hurt *you*." Maggie felt herself being squeezed farther and farther into that corner. "Your father is a man with many fine qualities, but most important of all, he loves you. You had a good time today—I won't believe otherwise."

"Okay, I did, but it was in spite of him, not because of him. I like to swim. Is that a crime?"

"You also like your father, and that's no crime, either. Why don't you give him a break?"

"Like you did?" Blair sneered. Her expression grew crafty. "If you like him so much, prove it."

"I thought I was."

"Ha!"

"Okay, what'll convince you? I went to Glenwood Springs with you, didn't I?"

"Yeah, and then ignored us."

"I did not. I just tried to let the two of you get better acquainted."

"You tried to avoid him—not that I blame you. No, it has to be something better than that...."

Quick alarm flared in Maggie's chest. "Like what?"

Blair shrugged too casually. "I don't know, but I'll think of something."

"WHAT DO YOU MEAN, who am I trying to fool?"

"I mean you're not getting away with it, Daddy. You don't like Maggie any better than you did in the beginning. So why are you pretending?"

Chase had thought the trip to Glenwood Springs at least a modest success; for one thing, he'd laughed with his daughter for the first time since she'd moved to Aspen. He also felt he'd gotten to know Maggie a lot better.

Now this. "What is it you think I'm pretending?" he asked cautiously.

"As if you don't know!" She glared at him. "You're pretending to like Maggie of course. You might as well give it up, though. I know what you're up to."

Hell, *he* didn't even know what he was up to. "Would you care to enlighten me, then?" When she gave him a blank look, he added, "What is it you think I'm up to?"

"I think you're pretending to like each other because you think that'll make points with me, but you can forget it. I see right through you!"

"But I really have changed my mind about Maggie. Now that I've gotten to know her better—"

"You don't know her at all. Why bother, Daddy? She's not your type."

Chase blinked in surprise. "My type? What do you think my type is?"

She let out a scornful sniff. "Don't play dumb, okay? You like blondes with big—"

"All right already!" He felt as if she'd punched him in the gut. He'd been so careful—or had he? Had he just thought she was too young to notice, too innocent to figure out what was going on?

"You've got me all wrong," he protested, but this was not a point he could vigorously defend.

"Whatever. Maggie's not your type, so why pretend you like her?"

"Maggie's a fine woman, Blair, and she's got your best interests at heart." He said it easily, because it was true. "The more I get to know her... well, the more I like her."

"That's what she says about you, and I don't believe either one of you." Blair gave an impatient toss of her head. "I liked it better when you were at each other's throats."

He just bet she did. "So what'll it take to convince you?"

A kind of crafty expression crossed her face. "I don't know," she said evasively. "When I figure it out, I'll let you know."

He just bet she would.

"So, DID YOU HAVE FUN at Glenwood Springs today, Blair?"

"Oh, Libby—" a mighty sigh "—it was okay, I guess. I wish you could've gone."

"Me, too. I'll bet your father's really hot in a swimsuit."

"Gross!"

"I'll bet Maggie agrees with me."

"That reminds me..."

"What?"

"Maggie and my father are up to something."

"Like what?"

"They're being too nice to each other."

"That's great! Oh, Blair, do you think they're in love?"

"Gross!"

"What then?"

"I think they're trying to put one over on me—you know, for my own good. Barf! But I can outsmart them."

"Wow, Blair, I love your tricky little mind."

Both girls giggled; then Blair said, "If they really all of a sudden like each other, they shouldn't mind going out on a date, right? If they won't, it'll prove what big liars they are."

"I guess so, but what's the point? I mean, like, why do you even care if they like each other or not?"

"Well, I think I see a way to get Daddy off my back."

"Huh?"

Blair shook her head impatiently. "Libby, I've got to get him married again."

Her friend gasped. "Oh, Blair, what if he married a witch-with-a-*b*? You really don't need a wicked stepmother."

"Take it easy. I can't lose on this one. If he marries a bitch, she'll be *glad* to send me to school in Switzerland. But if he marries Maggie—"

"Maggie? But you just said—"

"If he marries Maggie, she'll make him let me go to school in Switzerland because she's on my side. The best part of all is, no matter *who* he marries, he'll get off *my* back. Naturally I'd prefer Maggie to some strange bimbo, but I won't be around much, anyway. End of plan."

Silence settled over the phone line, and then Libby sighed. "I don't know, Blair. This sounds a little risky to me. If he gets on to you, he could ground you for *life.* Are you sure . . . ?"

Blair was very sure indeed.

AT BREAKFAST the next morning, Blair was the very model of a cheerful child. This turnabout surprised Maggie, and apparently Chase, as well, for he kept stealing curious looks at his daughter.

Blair finished the last bite of cereal in her bowl and laid down her spoon. "So," she said heartily, "I've been thinking about yesterday. . ."

Immediately Maggie's antenna went up. A glance at Chase confirmed that he, too, had gone on red alert.

". . . and maybe I was wrong."

Chase reached for another bran muffin. "About what?"

"About you and Maggie."

"Me and Maggie?" The notion seemed to amuse him.

"That's right." Blair's smile was ingratiating. "Maggie's a very likable person. I don't guess I can blame you for liking her, too."

Chase laughed out loud, and Maggie joined in somewhat reluctantly. "Good point," he conceded.

Blair frowned. "It's a little harder to figure out what Maggie sees in you, but maybe she agrees with Libby."

"What's Libby got to do with it?" Maggie wondered.

"She says Daddy's hot."

Blair spoke ingenuously, but Maggie didn't believe for a minute that the girl didn't know what she was saying. Heat swept up Maggie's cheeks; remembering Chase in his red swimsuit, she had to admit Libby was right on target with that one.

"Anyway," Blair went on as if unaware of the currents around her, "I'm almost convinced you guys aren't trying to do a number on me."

Chase grinned. "Sweetheart, Maggie and I have just . . . well, come to like and respect each other, that's all."

"In that case," Blair responded without missing a beat, "when are the two of you going out on a date?"

"A date!" Maggie stared at Chase, aghast. What was the child thinking?

"Hey, we're friends, nothing more," Chase objected.

"If it's really a friendship, how could going out on a date hurt it?" Blair countered. She sucked in a breath. "I was starting to believe you. But if you can't even stand the thought of a friendly little dinner, just the two of you . . ."

She looked so sad that Maggie's already guilty conscience kicked in. "You just don't understand, Blair.

Your father and I have a...a business friendship, I guess you'd say. Dating would just...just..." *Help me out here, Chase,* she implored with her eyes.

"Complicate things," he put in quickly. "When you get a little older—"

"I'm old enough to know when I've been had." Lips pressed tightly together, Blair slammed her napkin onto the table and stalked from the room.

MAGGIE GROANED. "I'm sorry! I had no idea she'd come up with anything so outlandish."

"Having dinner with me is outlandish?" He should be ashamed of himself, Chase thought, egging her on this way. But he didn't find the idea of spending a little time with Maggie all that alarming. It would give him a chance to delve more deeply into her secrets.

"You know what I mean." She glared at him. "What do you suppose she's up to?"

"It's obvious. She wants us to convince her we're sincere in our sudden declarations of mutual regard. If we don't, it's back to square one."

"I'm not so sure." Maggie looked thoughtful. "I wonder..." She shook her head suddenly. "No, she wouldn't be that calculating."

"So what do you say?"

"To her? I think it's up to you to talk to her. She's *your* daughter."

He shook his head. "I mean about going out to dinner. Maybe that would placate her."

"Us? You and me, dinner? Not a chance!"

"Why not?" he wheedled. "You can pick the place—sky's the limit."

"Absolutely not."

"What're you afraid of, Maggie?" He pinned her with his gaze, enjoying the heightened color on her cheeks, the confusion in the eloquent brown eyes. "I'll be a perfect gentleman, if that's what's worrying you."

"It's not."

"Then what?" He waited, watching the struggle on her usually composed face. "We're on the same side in this, you know."

"Are we?"

"I thought we were. Why would you question it?"

"Because I don't trust you as far as I can throw you. There, are you satisfied? I feel as if I'm perpetrating a hoax on your daughter, and it makes me very uncomfortable."

"Have you lied to her about my finer qualities? You said you wouldn't."

"I haven't lied to her."

"Then I must have some decent qualities."

"I never said you didn't."

"Then what's your problem, sweetheart?"

"*You*, sweetheart," she snapped. "I really dislike your patronizing attitude. I'm not one of your groupies, and I'm not impressed by your life-style."

"You're impressed by something," he guessed shrewdly. "What is it, Maggie? What is it about me that gets to you?" *For that matter, what is it about you that gets to me?*

"Don't flatter yourself."

"I seldom do." And this time, not at all, for he felt the connection between them as vividly as electrical currents arcing through the air. He was making her crazy, all right. Reminding her that she had sexual desires. Desires that needed quenching.

She stood up, her movements jerky and her breathing rapid. "I'm not going out with you and that's that," she announced in a voice that quivered. "I'd sooner face a firing squad than a date with you."

"But would you sooner disillusion a little girl who's just learning to trust?" he returned quickly. "Think about that, Maggie Colby. Just think about it."

SHE DID OF COURSE, despite all effort to the contrary. She thought she was doing all right, too—until Julie called late that afternoon.

"What in the world are you doing to that child?" Julie demanded. "She was crying so hard that—"

"Crying!" Filled with remorse, Maggie looked toward the kitchen, where Blair had gone for a soda. "She called you? I don't understand."

"I think she just wanted someone to talk to, and frankly, Maggie, she's not sure she can trust you anymore."

Maggie groaned. "But that's not fair! I—"

"Fair, shmair. She's just a little girl."

"Okay, tell me what she said."

"That you and her daddy are trying to trick her. It was hard to get the gist of it, but I gather she's got her heart set on the two of you being friends."

"But we *are* friends," Maggie wailed, crossing the fingers of one hand behind her back; it'd be a cold day in hell before she accepted Chase Britton as a friend.

"Yeah, like cats and dogs. What would it hurt you to go out to dinner with the man? It'd make Blair happy, and isn't that the point?"

"I suppose, but you don't underst—"

"One lousy dinner. You're such a hayseed, Maggie! I'd jump at the chance if it was me. I'd make him take me to the most expensive and exclusive place in town—"

"He *owns* the most expensive and exclusive place in town."

"Okay, then I'd make him take me to some local dive full of down-home music and good ol' boys. So you spend one crummy evening with a man you're not in love with, so what? Nobody's asking you to sleep with the guy, just make a little girl happy."

Sure sounded simple, put that way.

8

JULIE, BLAIR'S self-appointed baby-sitter, peered critically over her big sister's shoulder. "Why don't you wear your hair down?" she complained. "Why don't you undo just one more button on your shirt? Why don't you—"

"Why don't you get off my case?" Maggie was trembling; she couldn't believe she was doing this. She didn't even look like herself, thanks to Julie. The turquoise shirt, cut in Western lines, was too snug for peace of mind; so were the matching jeans. Julie had insisted on lending her a wide carved leather belt with pearl buckle, and a fringed buckskin jacket. Maggie had pulled her heavy hair back with a turquoise clip, a concession to an evening at the Painted Pony Saloon.

Chase would be out of his element there, she comforted herself, remembering another time at another saloon. He was a real city slicker. What was she afraid of?

"So far so good," Julie announced. "Now I'll do your makeup, and no back talk. No sister of mine is going to run around Aspen looking like a hick from the sticks."

Even if that's what she is, Maggie added silently.

WHAT MAGGIE HAD BEEN hiding beneath the shapeless items in her wardrobe was definitely nothing to be ashamed of. Meeting her in the living room beneath the sharp eyes of her sister and the suspicious eyes of his daughter, Chase freely admitted that.

Maggie Colby was all woman. Not for her the pencil-thin figure of fashion or the hard-muscled body achieved by hours with weight machines and personal trainers. Maggie was woman with a capital *W*, curvy and deep-breasted and broad-hipped, a small waist giving her a classic hourglass figure.

She took a quick breath and her cleavage deepened inside the open V of her shirt. "Damn," she muttered for his ears only. "It's like having your parents send you off to the prom." She rolled her eyes expressively.

He merely smiled, his mouth so dry he didn't trust himself to speak.

Not so, Julie Cameron. She stood at the front door, Blair at her side, to bid them farewell with a final word of advice: "Don't do anything I wouldn't do!"

Chase, who was getting his second wind, figured that covered a lot of territory.

THE DOWDY SCHOOLTEACHER had turned into a sexy butterfly, but she didn't seem to know it. Chase was less surprised by the transformation than by her apparent failure to realize how sensational she looked. He could tell she still felt insecure. The interested male glances she drew apparently did nothing to reassure her, or perhaps she didn't even notice them.

Was she for real?

The Painted Pony was Colorado with a vengeance. Unlike the Hideout in Cupid, which was the real thing, the Pony's ambience was studied and expensive. Nevertheless, he saw her begin to relax once they were seated in a booth upholstered in something approximating spotted horsehide.

They dined on barbecued ribs and drank beer, while Chase tried to stop thinking about dancing as something more than a means to feel those lush breasts against his chest. He got so worked up about the idea that he almost laughed at himself. Lord, what was he thinking?

They spoke of inconsequential things, although he'd intended to wheedle as much personal information out of her as he could. He was still too flummoxed by her physical presence to be subtle; that would have to wait for another day.

At last his raunchy thoughts got the better of him and he was on his feet, pulling her from the booth while the band played some country ballad about lost loves and pickup trucks. She resisted, glancing around uncomfortably as if she feared making a fool of herself. Adroitly he spun her in a graceful arc and into his arms.

Damn, it was like shoving a finger into an electrical socket—only it wasn't his finger that reacted when she came up hard against him, their bodies meeting chest to knee. She gave him a startled wide-eyed look, but didn't try to pull away.

Even if she'd tried, she wouldn't have succeeded, for he held her closely and danced her in a breathtaking circle, just as if he wasn't tight as a corkscrew. By the time he slowed the pace, he'd regained at least partial control.

Enough, anyway, to lift his head and grin down at her. "I told you once that line-dancing wasn't my thing," he murmured. Before she could reply, he cupped her head with one hand and pressed her cheek against the skin beneath the open collar of his shirt. For a long time, they communicated in the dance while sexual tension continued to grow. By the time they got back to Chase's house, it was so thick you could almost taste it.

MAGGIE STOOD at the foot of the stairs leading to her bedroom on the second floor, her mind in a daze and her body in an uproar. What could she have been thinking to dance with him that way?

Hell, the same thing she was thinking now. She clutched her hands together behind her back to keep from grabbing him.

"Aw, come on, it wasn't all that bad," Chase teased.

He laid his hands on her shoulders, and she quivered in reaction, yet felt helpless to step away. He seemed to understand instinctively how to touch her, how to handle her. But he managed to do it so casually, so naturally, that resistance wasn't even an option.

"I had a...nice time," she admitted, her voice strained. "You're a very good dancer."

"One of many talents."

Despite the lightness of his tone, he looked at her with an intensity that sent prickles of excitement up her spine. She couldn't guess if he intended to kiss her or shake her hand—and wasn't at all sure which farewell she'd prefer. The thought of his lips on hers made her knees weak, but after the way he'd held her in his arms, wouldn't a handshake be the equivalent of a slap in the face?

Okay, that had been on a dance floor; otherwise he'd been a perfect gentleman. But her breasts still throbbed and tightened as if retaining the imprint of his chest, and her stomach clenched with the memory of . . .

He was putting out his hand, and she'd have to put her own into it. He'd thank her for helping deceive his daughter, and that would be that. Tomorrow this would seem unreal; unlike Cinderella, she wouldn't even have a missing glass slipper to remind her.

His gaze, so strong on hers, wavered finally, lifted as if in search of divine guidance. He sighed and his hand closed over hers.

"What the hell," he muttered—and yanked her into his arms so hard it knocked the breath out of her.

Before she could regain her senses, his mouth covered hers. For a shocked instant she hesitated, but for the life of her, she couldn't dredge up the will to resist. A gasp parted her lips and his tongue thrust between her teeth, sending a fiery explosion of pleasure through her veins. She wound her arms around his neck, pressing her aching breasts against his chest, thinking she'd never wanted any man the way she wanted this one.

Had she dreamed of that first kiss they'd shared so long ago, all the time between? Had that single kiss, the one that should never have happened because she'd been a married woman, stood between her and any kind of relationship even after her widowhood?

He pulled back, breathing heavily. She groaned and swayed toward him, her eyes squeezed tightly closed. But his hands on her arms held her away, and after a moment, she realized something had changed. With an effort, she forced her heavy eyelids to open.

He was looking at her in the strangest way, almost as if he expected her to ... what? Slap his face? Confused, she leaned away from him, clutching a newel post for support.

He cleared his throat, not looking quite like his usual urbane self. "So you saw her, too," he said cautiously.

"Wh-who?" Maggie glanced around in utter bewilderment, the truth dawning in a terrible rush. *Blair!* The girl must have been watching from the top of the stairs—maybe Julie, too. Maggie bit her lip; had anyone ever died from humiliation?

"Of course," she blurted the lie. "Wh-why else would I ... I mean, you don't think ..."

"No. No, of course not." Chase backed away as if he couldn't wait to make his escape. "Uh ... thanks for everything. I mean, the evening and ... and—" his glance swept up the stairway "—everything."

She'd never seen him so rattled. She wanted to take advantage of that unusual state of affairs by responding with a light "Hey, anytime," but there was always the chance he might try to take her up on it. Not that she'd ever put herself in a position like this again.

With a brusque nod, she turned her back on him and tried to run up the stairs. Unfortunately her knees were so mushy that if she hadn't had a banister to cling to, she might not have made it at all.

"SO, HOW WAS your evening?"

Julie's grin over her coffee cup was Cheshire-cat crafty. Had she, as well as Blair, seen that fiery goodnight kiss? Maggie felt her cheeks burn with mortification. "The evening was . . . okay," she said with a dismissive shrug.

"Just okay?" Julie's brows soared. "From what I saw—"

"So you *were* spying on us. For shame!"

"Ha! You didn't see me. You were turned the wrong way."

"Chase did. It's the same thing."

"Not exactly." Julie put down her cup. "Look, Maggie, I've got to hit the road. I'll go find Blair and say goodbye, but first, I've got something for you." Reaching into her purse, she pulled out her gift.

Maggie unfolded the strip of plasticized paper, which turned out to be a bright red bumper sticker that said, "Life is uncertain. Eat dessert first." "What's this supposed to mean?" she demanded.

"The second part means, never save the best for last," Julie interpreted blithely, "be it men or chocolate. I think you know what 'Life is uncertain' means."

Maggie did, to her grief. And to a woman celibate for a dozen years, Chase was beginning to seem not only like dessert but a twelve-course banquet.

And she was starving.

SHE WANTED to avoid him, but what could she do? Blair was too much on the alert; the first time Maggie tried to beg off on an outing, the girl leapt to the attack.

"Why won't you come if you're so crazy about him?"

"I never said I was crazy about him."

"But when I saw the two of you making out after your date—"

"Making out! We were doing no such thing—and why were you spying on us?"

"I wasn't spying, I was, uh, I thought I heard a burglar." Blair thrust out her lower lip. "I know making out when I see it."

"You saw a simple thank-you-for-a-lovely-evening kiss, that's all. It didn't mean any more than a . . . a handshake."

Blair glowered at her tutor. "I'll remind you of that when I start dating."

Maggie wanted to argue but realized her position wasn't a strong one. So, when pressed, she joined father and daughter on a search for a new summer wardrobe for Blair. With dozens of one-of-a-kind shops clustered in a five-block pedestrian mall downtown, there was plenty of choice—for those willing to pay the prices. Walking leisurely from door to door, poking their heads into shops that looked interesting, they made progress slowly.

At first Maggie felt ill at ease, but that soon disappeared, for Chase acted exactly as he always had. There were no lingering glances, no guilty starts. Obviously what had happened between them had meant exactly nothing to him.

It was only the country bumpkin who'd been thrown completely off her stride. Well, two could play this game, she decided, lifting her chin—at least during the day.

Nighttime was something else again.

CHASE KNEW he'd been out of line with that kiss, but he'd seen his chance and grabbed it. She'd been all he'd expected: soft and warm and oh-so-willing in his arms. Too much so, in fact. If he hadn't known Blair was watching . . .

Biting back a groan indicative of his growing tension and frustration, he held open the door to yet another boutique. Shopping was not his favorite thing in the best of circumstances; shopping for a kid was awful.

He'd like to be shopping for Maggie. He shot her a surreptitious glance, hating what he saw: jeans, an oversize smock of some sort concealing that zaftig body, beat-up cowboy boots. If he'd thought—

hoped—she'd stop her habit of hiding her assets after their date, he'd soon been disabused of that notion.

She looked up with a smile meant for his daughter, not him. "These are nice, Blair." She lifted a pair of shorts, glanced at the price tag, did a double take and dropped them like a hot potato.

Chase caught a glimpse of his own goofy grin in a mirrored wall and quickly wiped his face clean of expression. Maggie had never known plenty, not when it came to cold hard cash. Yet she wasn't the poorer for it; she was in many ways richer than he. It was asinine to pay almost a hundred dollars for a pair of khaki shorts for a twelve-year-old girl—or anyone, for that matter.

Except maybe for a woman whose legs you'd like to get a good look at . . .

A smiling pearl-draped saleslady approached Maggie. "Is your daughter looking for something in particular?" she inquired.

"Oh, she's not . . ." A red tide suffused Maggie's face and she glanced at Chase guiltily.

Blair had heard. "Mother!" She flung her arms around Maggie's waist and said to the salesclerk, "She always denies knowing me, but we look so much alike no one believes her."

Maggie laughed uncomfortably, trying to unwind the girl's arms. "She's teasing. Actually we're looking for—"

"Daddy!" Blair appealed to Chase. "Mother's trying to disown me again."

Chase stifled a grin. He'd rarely seen his daughter in
such a playful mood—or Maggie so discombobulated.
Putting his arm around Maggie's shoulders, he dropped
a quick kiss on her temple. She shot him a shocked
glance.

"Now, dear," he said soothingly, "I know she's a trial
to you, but I don't think they'll take her back."

"Chase!"

"Mommie!"

"Darling!"

"THAT WAS ROTTEN," Maggie announced self-
righteously, holding her ice-cream cone out so the
melting drips fell on the pavement, not on her.

"Silly, maybe," Chase said. "Not rotten."

He leaned forward to lick his own cone, and Maggie
turned away, her stomach clenching at the sight of his
tongue flicking out that way. "It was presumptuous,"
she said flatly, "and you've already presumed far too
much, Chase. It's got to stop."

He strolled around in front of her, and again she
turned to avoid facing him. Her glance sought out Blair,
among a small crowd of children enthralled by the an-
tics of a street mime.

"Presumed, huh?" He sounded thoughtful. "That
means you're pissed off because of the kiss, right?"

"No! Well, yes, that and other... things." *Like the
way you come to breakfast every morning half-dressed,
and that lazy sexy smile when you're making a point,
and a whole lot more.*

He cocked his head, watching her. "If you think I'm going to apologize for the kiss or anything else, you're dead wrong. I thought it was . . . pretty nice. I enjoyed our evening together, and I think you did, too."

"Oh, Chase, that's not the point." She looked down miserably at her melting cone.

"Meaning you did enjoy it, but you won't admit it."

"Meaning I'm not going to mince words with you, because you'll win. You always win—winning's what you do best. I'm not in your league and I don't want to be. The day I don't flinch at hundred-dollar shorts is a day I don't want to see. Our values are different—"

"Maybe not as different as you think."

"—and our backgrounds are different. I want you to keep your distance. No, I'm *ordering* you to keep your distance."

His eyes narrowed and his mouth curved up. "That almost sounds like a challenge."

"It's not. It's a warning. Keep away from me or I'm gone. Is that plain enough for you? I'm not one of your groupies."

"I don't have any groupies." He looked astonished that she'd think so.

"Whatever." Taking a few steps to the curb, she dropped her cone into a trash receptacle. "Hands off, buster."

"I never go where I'm not wanted," he said grandly. He popped the last bit of cone into his mouth and licked his lips.

And once again she had to turn away.

A WEEKEND AT HOME on the ranch should have made Maggie feel better, but it didn't. Ben was on a tear because two hands had quit without notice and Jason was out rodeoing when he was needed. Julie, who was a pretty fair hand herself, was in Denver for some kind of journalism symposium. Granny was down with a bad summer cold, which also had Joey and Lisa Marie sniffling and whining, which meant Betsy had her hands full as nurse, chief cook and bottle washer.

For the first time in her life, Maggie felt like the odd man out in her own home. The feeling was so strong that she actually cut short her visit, deciding to return to Aspen Sunday evening, instead of Monday morning.

It didn't seem to her that anyone was particularly sorry to see her go, although when she headed for the car, Betsy followed.

"I'm so sorry, Maggie." Betsy pushed curly hair away from her forehead and sighed. "We've hardly had a chance to talk."

"You're busy. I understand."

"You *are* getting along with Chase all right, aren't you? You haven't said much, but I think I caught a little undercurrent there."

Maggie shrugged noncommittally. On a sudden impulse, she asked, "Betts, did you ever meet his wife?"

Betsy shook her head. "They'd split way before he and I became friends. I understand she was a real . . . shark."

"Did you ever, you know, have a romantic relationship with him?"

"Good heavens, no!" Betsy looked shocked at the very idea. Then her eyes went wide. "Do you realize if Chase hadn't invited me to Aspen, I'd never have met Ben?" Her smile turned luminous. "Which is another way of saying, I owe Chase Britton a lot."

She rose on tiptoe and planted a kiss on her sister-in-law's cheek. "I owe you a lot, too. I hope everything's working out for you this summer, Maggie. I'm a little ashamed of the way we all kind of pushed you into this job. You're not sorry, are you?"

Maggie sighed. Was she sorry?

"Because," Betsy went on thoughtfully, "I've discovered that the things I regret are almost always the things I didn't have the nerve to try and almost never the things I tried but didn't work out."

"In other words, do something even if you do it wrong," Maggie murmured, and she wasn't thinking about Betsy.

She was thinking about a man, a man who was driving her crazy.

BETSY STOOD in the ranch driveway watching Maggie's old rattletrap till it was out of sight. Ben walked out of the barn, brushing hay from his jeans.

"Wanna give me a hand in here?" he asked brusquely, as if she should have known he needed her without being told.

"In a minute." She turned toward the house with sudden determination. "First I want to call Blair Britton..."

THE HOUSE WAS DARK, the only glimmer of light a ghostly glow coming from the pool area out back. Leaving her small suitcase beside the stairs, Maggie walked slowly down the hall as if drawn by some magnetic force.

Her heart was pounding; she wasn't sure why, although she supposed it had something to do with the tumultuous thoughts Betsy's final comments had stirred up. It was true; Maggie rarely regretted the things she'd done, even those that turned out badly—like her marriage. She'd loved Chuck, and she didn't even want to think about what his life would have been like after his accident without her to care for him. It had been difficult, but she didn't regret it, never had.

But she'd often regretted the things she'd never had the opportunity or the guts to try, things like love affairs and travel to exotic places and motherhood. Now she was thirty-five years old. Thirty-five. It seemed like a hundred, because the decade leading up to it had been little more than endless work and endless worry. She felt over-the-hill, washed-up, used up, out of it. Except when she was with—

"Hello."

At the soft greeting, she froze, little tremors of excitement shooting through her. "H-hello." She spotted Chase at one end of the pool, a towel draped over his lap and his feet dangling in the water. The blue underwater light cast that eerie glow, almost making her feel as if she'd entered another dimension.

His voice sounded muted and distant. "I didn't expect you until tomorrow."

"My plans changed." She licked her lips and looked around. "Where's Blair?"

He stood up carefully, bringing the towel with him. The white terry cloth looked almost fluorescent against his skin. A gap on one hip told her that beneath the small towel there was nothing whatsoever except . . . man. Bare, naked man.

"Blair's spending the night at Libby's," he said in that same disembodied voice. The towel rode lower over his flat belly and he clutched it with both hands. "The invitation came up rather suddenly, but I saw no reason not to let her go. We were at each other's throats all weekend—she's on that Switzerland kick again—so it seemed like a good idea, since you weren't going to be here. Only here you are . . ."

"Yes," she murmured, "here I am." She swallowed hard. "I . . . I guess I should leave you to it." She gestured toward the pool but made no move to leave.

"Maggie." His gaze locked with hers. "Don't go. I . . . You're like the answer to a prayer."

"I'm sorry?"

"Don't pretend you don't understand. I was thinking about you." He paused, then, "Damn, Maggie, you're driving me nuts! I want you so bad my teeth ache. Do you want me back?" He stared at her with hot intensity. "Say something, dammit."

For a sizzling moment she met his gaze. Yes, she wanted him—but did she have the guts to act on it? If she didn't, she suddenly realized, she'd never be able to forgive herself. Opportunities like this didn't come along every day, not to ordinary women like her.

She sucked in a breath. "There must be something in the air tonight because I feel . . ."

He took a step toward her, his broad chest expanding. In the shadowy light, his cheekbones were works of art, his mouth a sensual curve. "It's not in the air— it's in the blood. It's in *our* blood, Maggie, beautiful, beautiful Maggie. There are so many things I want to say to you...do to you and with you...do for you..."

"Then drop that silly towel," she said in a strangled voice, "and *show* me, Chase. Just this once, before I lose my nerve."

The towel hit the tiles.

9

NUDITY HAD NEVER BEEN a problem for Chase. He was
comfortable with his body and with the bodies of others, accepting and uncritical. He'd made love to women
whose bodies were the envy and desire of millions, and
women with more modest attributes, but rarely found
one more exceptional than another—except in terms of
responsiveness.

He already knew from past experience that Maggie
Colby's body was one of the most responsive. Standing before her, naked as the day he was born, he reached
out to touch her breasts. Her chin dropped onto her
chest and she stood there trembling. And looking at
him, at the evidence of his desire for her, rising from the
thicket of hair between his thighs.

He unbuttoned her blouse and she didn't resist, although she didn't help, either; she stood almost as if in
a trance. He slid the smooth fabric from her shoulders,
and she lifted her arms just enough to let the garment
slip to the deck. She wore a plain white cotton bra,
which barely contained her full breasts.

She licked her lips, daring a quick glance up at his
face. "I feel…funny about this," she whispered. "Aren't
you at least going to kiss me?"

"Yes. But I've waited so damned long for this I'm afraid—" he unsnapped her jeans with a quick jerk that made her gasp "—if I kiss you before I undress you—" he stepped closer to shove her jeans down "—I might end up disgracing myself."

"You haven't waited *that* long," she objected, zeroing in on the inconsequential.

Her lush body emerged by inches from the rough denim. The bra dropped past his downcast vision, and he realized she'd removed it herself. Those delicious breasts were unfettered, but he didn't dare look up quite yet. She deserved an answer while he was still capable of making one.

He stroked her hips. "I think I've been waiting since that night I walked you home from the Hideout."

"Y-you didn't walk me home. You walked me to—"

"I don't give a damn where I walked you. It's the kiss I couldn't forget."

The jeans hit the deck and she stepped out of them and her shoes at the same time—loafers, not boots, for once. She stood before him, wearing nothing but plain cotton panties, her arms crossed over her breasts, creating even deeper cleavage. She trembled, her face filled with an eager apprehension that went through him like a bolt of lightning.

"You've never done this before," he said suddenly.

She gasped. "Of course I have. I was a married woman."

He held himself back with great effort. "That's not what I mean. Have you ever had sex with a man you weren't married to?"

She flinched. "I've never *had* sex, not the way you mean. I've made love . . ."

She wasn't comfortable talking about such things, but he was insistent. "With your husband." He stroked her shoulder.

She arched beneath his hand, exquisitely responsive. "Yes. Call me old-fashioned." She looked almost ashamed. "But that . . . was a long time ago, Chase. If I'm not very good at this, please be patient."

"You're going to be wonderful at this," he assured her, stroking down until his palms touched the forearms shielding her breasts. Gently he grasped her wrists and drew her arms wide. "You're beautiful," he whispered, filled with awe at the truth of this observation.

"I'm not," she protested miserably. "I'm too big in some places and not big enough in others. I'm—"

"Perfect."

He closed his hands around the warm swell of her breasts and lifted. She sighed and leaned into the kneading motions of his hands. The last speck of uncertainty flowed out of her, and she purred like a cat. "Yes," she sighed. "Touch me like that. I've wanted..."

And so had he, he thought, bending to draw a nipple deep into his mouth. He swirled his tongue around the beaded tip and suckled strongly before moving to the other breast. Her own hands covered his ears, pulling him closer.

Dropping to his knees, he kissed the gentle mound of her belly, then thrust a hand beneath the elastic of her panties, exploring the throbbing triangle between her thighs and parting the silky cluster of tight curls. She shuddered at the touch, her breath coming in ragged gasps.

Beneath the panties, she was wet and ready—and they hadn't even kissed, he thought with a kind of dizzy wonder. He was going about this all wrong, backward, but it was working. He continued to stroke her and felt the shiver race through her body even before she cried out.

He had to have her then, flat on her back under him in the most basic way. Rising, he claimed her mouth at last. She opened her lips for him, sliding her arms around him and kissing him back as if she'd never get enough. He slid his knee between her legs, and his tense thigh pressed into her dampness. She clung to him, letting him guide her backward, until her feet struck the air mattress at the edge of the pool.

Holding her by the elbows, his mouth still dominating hers, he lowered her. For a moment he looked into her passion-glazed face, seeing the half-closed eyes, the half-opened lips.

This need to possess her overwhelmed him. A part of his mind knew he wasn't prepared—he had no protection for her—but he'd lost all self-control. He, a man who always knew what he was doing and did it with care and deliberation, had nothing except a raging need to lose himself in her, consequences be damned.

Whatever the price, he would pay it. He moved over her, covered her, positioned himself for the uniting thrust. Reckless abandon flooded through his veins like lava.

He felt, in that instant, like a king.

MAGGIE TWINED her legs around his waist and lifted her hips. His entry was less an invasion than an inevitable conclusion long desired, yet barely imaginable in its splendor. To be penetrated and filled so completely that fierce intoxicating pleasure spiraled through her, consuming her . . .

He sought her mouth, at the same time beginning to move inside her. Smooth strokes became deeper and more powerful. Effortlessly she adjusted to his pace, their passions tangling into a hot skein of mindless sensuality. Twisting her head on the mattress, she moaned his name and grabbed his heaving shoulders, her nails biting into the skin.

The force of her orgasm tore a cry from her throat, and her body convulsed around him. Her sweet release was echoed by his own, and his answering cry was hoarse and triumphant.

They lay in the moonlight, still joined, trying to regain their breath and their senses. Then, with a sigh that might have been regret, Chase rolled over onto the mat beside her. She turned her head to look at him, no longer ashamed of her nudity or what had passed between them.

Chase Britton really was the handsomest man she'd ever known, the most sophisticated and certainly the wealthiest. But none of that was important. What mattered was that he had somehow managed—cared enough?—to penetrate her mask to find the vulnerable needy woman she really was.

She'd thought her life was over. She'd thought she'd never feel this way again, safe and loved and *whole*. But one wild sexual encounter, no matter how intensely satisfying, could not erase her deeper inadequacies. If only...

She looked at him, naked beside her, and prayed he'd say something, anything, that would tell her he understood even a little of what she was feeling. Sitting up with a sigh, she drew her knees up and circled them with her arms, feeling suddenly awkward.

He stretched, his body a sinewy sculpture of light and shadow. "Was it good for you, too?" he murmured, his face breaking into a wolfish grin. "If you're not sure, we can always have another go at it."

He reached out to draw one hand languidly down her curved spine, but he might as well have punched her in the gut.

HE HARDLY KNEW what hit him. One minute he was trying to break an awkward silence with a lighthearted suggestion. The next he was staring after her retreating form.

Her beautiful and furious retreating form.

She'd called him a bastard, jumped to her feet and stalked off. Hell, he hadn't meant to offend her. He knew damned well it'd been good for her, probably at least as good as it had been for him. But he wasn't above garnering a few huzzahs.

He was only human, after all.

Dropping back on the mat, he bent his arms and pillowed his head with his hands to stare up at the stars. He felt both hollow and full to overflowing. He'd thought that once they had sex—made love, she'd corrected him—they'd enter a more mutually satisfying phase of their relationship.

So why was she so bent out of shape? Hell, did she think once would be enough? Was the idea of doing it again, perhaps a little differently, so offensive?

He sat up, shoving his hair back with both hands. He'd known they were attracted to each other that first night in Cupid. He'd wanted to act on that attraction even then. In the intervening years, he'd relegated her to the status of minor irritation, convincing himself that she was not his kind of woman. Now, as he lay staring at the stars, he could see he'd been right. If she *had* been his kind of woman, she'd be here right now, letting him lead her into all kinds of sensual adventures.

Sweating, he realized he was getting all worked up again. Damn her. She had no right to start something she wasn't willing to finish.

What the hell had she expected? A marriage proposal?

IT HAD MEANT nothing to him. He'd made a joke of it. Maggie could have stood just about anything but that, after giving him everything she had to give. His idea of humor cut her to the quick and left her without a shred of dignity.

How could she face him now? Humiliated and hurting, she decided she'd simply have to keep her head high and do her job. And if Mr. Chase Britton so much as looked at her crosswise, she'd . . .

Quit and go home. That would be the only thing left for her, no matter how attached she'd become to Blair. Chase had exploited her weakness. She'd lusted after his body, but what she really wanted was him—all of him, not just a tumble beneath the stars.

She loved him. She hated him, but she loved him more. She'd been fighting an insane attraction since the night they'd met. She'd been weak but it would never ever happen again. She didn't need to beat herself up about it. She was a grown woman; this was the nineties.

So why did she feel as cheap as a two-dollar necktie?

LIFE IN THE BRITTON household went on, but not easily. For Blair's sake, Maggie made an effort and supposed Chase did, too, although in his case it could have been simple indifference.

She should be so lucky. Every time she looked at him her breasts tingled and heat curled in the pit of her stomach. When she closed her eyes at night, she saw him in all his naked magnificence; when she dreamed, she dreamed of him, their bodies intimately joined and their hearts beating as one.

He tried to talk to her about what had happened, but she refused to listen. If he apologized, she didn't think she'd be able to stand it. If his defense was pure insensitivity, she didn't think she could stand that, either.

So she stuck to Blair like glue, or stayed in her own room with a book, or took long walks through the pine and aspen, but under no circumstances did she spend a single minute alone with Chase Britton.

AT FIRST Chase was puzzled; then he felt the first flickers of anger. As ridiculous as it seemed, he began to wonder if the luscious but cantankerous Maggie Colby had simply used him to break her sexual fast.

Why that possibility upset him, he couldn't imagine, yet it did. He brooded over it for weeks, and then decided to do the only thing he could to restore his battered psyche.

"MORE CHAMPAGNE?" Jessica Grant lifted the dark green bottle.

Chase held out his crystal flute and she did the honors. When golden bubbles spilled over onto his hand, she leaned down quickly and her little pink tongue flicked out to whisk away the wine.

"Mmm." She licked glossy red lips. "Just as good as I remember."

Almost embarrassed, Chase slugged down the expensive wine, realized what he was doing and choked to a flustered halt.

Jessica's pleasant smile betrayed confusion. "Is anything wrong?"

"Wrong? What could possibly be wrong?" *I've slept with you a dozen times—no big deal. I know exactly what you like and vice versa. I could've phoned it in.*

"I don't know." She set her glass on the deck railing and turned to him, stepping close to press her hips against his. "Whatever it is, maybe this will help."

It was why he'd come here to her place. He waited for his body to react. Jessica was a beautiful sophisticated woman who'd forgotten more about sex than Maggie would ever— Damn, he hadn't meant to let that name intrude on his mindless pleasure. He moved his hips against Jessica's—and waited for his body to react.

"I've missed you, baby," she murmured. "I thought you'd never call."

He lifted his champagne glass behind her head and sipped, still waiting for his body to react. "I've been busy."

"We're *all* busy." She fumbled with his belt buckle. "Some things are . . . important enough . . ."

"Damn! I just remembered..." He set his glass on the railing and stepped away from her, his hands flying to repair the damage she'd done to his shirt and belt. "I've got an appointment and I'm late already. I'm afraid I have to—"

"An appointment!" She shoved her hands onto her hips and glared at him. "It's almost one in the morning! You wasted an entire evening with food and dancing, and now that we're about to see some action—"

"Another time." He edged toward the door. "I'll call."

"You liar. You won't call!" She stamped a foot. *"What is your problem, Chase Britton?"*

There was no way to tell her he was still waiting for his body to react. Damn that Maggie Colby.

BLAIR LOOKED ANGRILY across the breakfast table at her father and her tutor. "What's the matter with you guys now?" she demanded. "First you hate each other's guts, then you're best buds, and now you're acting like you hate each other again."

Chase slammed down his coffee cup in an extraordinary—for him—display of temper, which he immediately regretted. "Who's acting?" He cast a baleful glance at Maggie.

And felt his body react, when two days ago he couldn't *buy* a hard-on.

Maggie gave him the coldest, most quelling, most superior glance he'd yet received. "Your father and I agreed to disagree," she said.

"No, we didn't," he shot back. "How can we disagree when you won't talk to me?"

"I talk to you every single day." Her tone warned him not to push the issue. To Blair she said, "Today we're going to work on probability. Are you ready to—"

Chase leaned forward. "Dammit, Maggie, I'm sick of living in an armed camp."

"I can be packed and out of here in fifteen minutes."

"Not if I lock all the doors until you listen to me."

"There's nothing you can say that I'd care to hear."

Blair's head turned from one adult to the other as she followed the dispute like a tennis match. Suddenly her eyes went wide. "I get it now! You guys are crazy about each other!"

"What?" Both adults stared at her.

She nodded vigorously. "I see what's going on. It's just like in movies and books. When a man and a woman hate each other, it really means they're in love."

Maggie looked aghast. "Oh, sweetheart, you're wrong!"

"She doesn't even like me," Chase put in indignantly.

"I like you as much as you like me," Maggie shot back, obviously unwilling to let him lay all the blame at her feet.

"No, you don't," he countered. "You don't like me as much, and you sure as hell don't like me in the same way."

"You . . . you rat!" She was practically sputtering. "How dare you insinuate—" She stopped short, her beautiful velvet eyes opening wide.

Blair looked interested. "Insinuate what? Have I missed something?"

Maggie's cheeks turned the most glorious shade of crimson. "Of course not. It's been a long summer—"

"A long *hot* summer," Chase interjected.

"I'll accept that. But, Blair, I'm tired. I want to go back to my own home, get ready for school to open next month. You must be tired, too. You've worked hard. Your father—" she shot him a scathing glance "—should be very proud of you."

Blair's eyes grew round and anxious. "You mean you're really going to leave me?"

"You knew all along this was just for the summer."

"But I thought—" The girl bit her lip.

"What?" Chase was struck by a sudden horrifying thought. "Surely you didn't think—"

"Why not?" Blair tossed her head and glared at him. "If you got married—"

"Married!" Maggie exclaimed.

"Well, sure." Blair fidgeted in her seat. "Why not? I know you're both pretty old and stuff—"

Maggie groaned and Chase choked.

"—but there's no law saying old people can't get married, is there?"

"None that I know of," Chase conceded, "if they're stupid enough to want to. We're not. Tell her, Maggie."

She gave him a frosty grimace that could never pass for a smile. To Blair she said, "What's this all about? You're up to something."

"Well—" the girl looked down at the breakfast bar and picked at a toast crumb "—I think Daddy needs a wife."

"What for?" Chase roared.

"To bring joy and comfort to your old age," Blair replied sweetly. "And because if you had a wife to worry about, you might let me go to school in Switzerland!"

So there it was, gauntlet thrown again.

"NEVER! YOU'LL GO to Switzerland over my dead body."

"Works for *me*."

"You've got a smart mouth on you, kid."

"So? I just won't lie and pretend like you do."

"I've never lied to you. Name one lie I ever told you."

"You mean, besides you care anything about me?"

"I *do* care about you. You're my daughter and I love you. How am I ever going to make you understand—"

"Did you lie when you said you *like* Maggie or when you said you *don't?*"

"I . . . I like Maggie."

"Liar! You hate her guts. I heard her crying in her room, and I bet you made her do it. You hate *my* guts, too. You're just keeping me here to torture me!"

She burst into tears. Maggie, who'd sat frozen through the exchange, put her arms around the girl's quaking shoulders. "There, there, sweetheart, it'll be okay." She smoothed back the tangled brown hair. "Your father really does love you."

"Yeah, right," the girl sniffed. "Like he loves you? Yeah, right."

"Blair . . ," Chase dropped to his knees in front of his daughter. When he tried to put his hand on her arm, she shrank away. "Blair, I won't let you go to school in Switzerland because I want you here with me. I want to get to know you, and I want you to get to know me. You're my own flesh and blood. I—"

"No!" Blair sprang to her feet, eyes flashing through her tears. "You *don't* love me, you never loved me, and that's fine with me because I hate you! The only way you can prove anything different is to let me go!"

Weeping hysterically, she rushed from the room. Maggie felt sick. Warily she looked at Chase, something she'd avoided doing for some time now.

He stood up, thrust his hands into the pockets of his white shorts and rocked back on his heels. "She cares more about you than she does me," he said in a low frustrated tone.

"No, Chase! She's . . . mixed-up. She's trying to find out how far she can push you."

"Not to Switzerland, that's for sure."

"I understand how you feel, but maybe you might consider—"

"No, dammit!"

He moved so suddenly she had no chance to get beyond his reach. His hands settled on her shoulders and he jerked her forward, staring down into her shocked face. "I'm her father and I'm not giving up on her. Either you can back me on that or . . ."

His words trailed off, but she knew what he was telling her: *Back me or get the hell out of here.* "I've always backed you," she said, resentful that she had to give such reassurance. Even if they weren't getting along very well, he should realize she was a woman of principle.

"I'm sorry," he said stiffly, allowing his arms to drop away. "I apologize. It's just that…" He thrust his hands through his hair. "I've got to go do some serious thinking. You'll be here when I get back?"

"Of course." Maggie followed him toward the door. "What . . . what should I tell her if she asks about you?"

"Hell, Maggie." He stopped and once more looked into her eyes, his own dark and turbulent. "Do what you always do. Tell her the truth."

The tone of his parting shot was anything but pleasant.

10

BLAIR EMERGED from her room hours later, looking grim. "Tell the truth," she said bluntly to Maggie. "What do you *really* think of my father?"

"I think he loves you and I think he'll learn to be a pretty decent father, if you'll give him half a chance."

The girl shook her head impatiently. "That's not what I mean. How do *you* feel about him? Do you love him?"

"Blair! You can't go around asking personal questions like that."

"Why not? Because I'm a kid? Grown-ups do it all the time. Somebody's always asking *me* how I feel, then telling me how I *ought* to feel."

"It's not the same thing."

"It is, too. Will you *please* answer my question?"

"I certainly will not." Maggie busied herself by opening the refrigerator door, pulling out a can of diet soda, closing the door. Blair waited impatiently.

"Look," Maggie said, "I wouldn't tell you if I *hated* him, either. I simply won't talk about your father."

Blair nodded slowly. "I think you just did," she said.

MAGGIE SOON LEARNED Blair was an even better student than she'd thought. The girl had her tutor's icy stare and touch-me-not demeanor down pat. Being on the receiving end, Maggie soon learned, was not a lot of fun.

The day dragged on. Chase didn't return and he didn't call. Blair refused to crack open a book, and Maggie didn't have the stomach to force a showdown. While the girl splashed in the pool, Maggie tried to keep her mind off the mess she'd helped create.

Could Blair really have thought her father might marry her tutor? It'd be laughable—if it didn't hurt so much.

Blair ate dinner sullenly and disappeared into her room. Maggie saw her talking on the telephone, but when she glanced over and saw she had an audience, she got up and slammed the door in Maggie's face. In a few minutes the boom box came on loud and stayed on loud.

At eleven Maggie eased open the girl's door and found her sound asleep, the light on and the radio still blaring. She turned both off and slipped back into the hall. Now what? Chase hadn't returned yet, and Maggie was too wound up and worried to sleep.

Perhaps a cup of cocoa would help. She went downstairs to the kitchen. Without turning on the overhead light, she opened the refrigerator and peered inside. The voice behind her almost scared her out of ten years' growth.

"We've got to stop meeting like this."

She slammed the door, but before she could confront him, his arms closed around her from behind, his hands sliding up her midriff to cover her breasts. Shocked and enthralled, she was incapable of resistance.

"Oh, Maggie," he moaned tiredly, rubbing his cheek against the nape of her neck. "What am I going to do about her?"

She stood there and let him nuzzle her neck, massage her breasts beneath the soft fabric of her oversize T-shirt, pull her back against him until she felt the heat of his erection. She wanted desperately to believe she was only responding to his need for comfort, but knew that was a bald-faced lie.

She was responding to her own needs, both sexual and emotional. She wanted to share everything with him, good and bad. She wanted to be in his arms, in his heart. With every fiber of her being, she wished Blair's instincts were correct, that this man might want a future with her.

But hope and belief didn't always mesh.

Still, she had to offer what comfort she could. "It'll be all right," she said. Her voice had a husky tremor. She closed her arms over his, hungry for his touch. His hands lifted and kneaded the resilient flesh of her breasts, while his penis pressed against her bottom like an iron bar. She leaned back, her head falling onto his shoulder in a gesture of surrender.

"Will it be all right . . . ever?" He kissed her ear, his breath hot and moist. "Without you to mediate . . . You're not really going to leave us, are you? Stay, Maggie. I—we need you. Surely you know that."

All she really knew was how much she needed him. He stroked a hand down her rib cage, fingers splaying over the gentle curve of her belly to press her back even more tightly against him. Desire pooled in the pit of her stomach. She couldn't breathe, couldn't think.

And she couldn't say what he wanted to hear. "I can't stay," she whispered, covering his hand with hers to hold it nearer her beating heart. "I have my own life, and people . . . people who . . ."

"Maggie Colby," he said, his tongue flicking out to explore the whorls of her ear, "I'm going to do everything in my power to make you change your mind— starting now."

Heaven help her, she was willing to let him try.

HIS BED WAS practically a stage, a huge cushy nest on a platform in the middle of the enormous room. She glanced up, almost expecting to see a mirror on the ceiling.

He noticed. "I'm not a voyeur," he murmured while they undressed each other between breathless kisses and caresses, "although I do like to see what I'm doing—and what's being done to me."

She reached for him, her hand curving around his engorged length. He went still and his gaze met hers, sultry and sizzling with passion. She slid her hand down his silken hardness, entranced by the feel of him.

He sucked in a ragged breath and his hand circled her wrist, halting her motion. It took him a moment to regain control. Once he did, he lifted her easily into his arms and lowered her onto the bed. She parted her thighs, and with a sigh he settled into the cradle she'd formed, only to rise quickly onto his knees.

"Not yet." His throaty voice was muffled against her skin as he rained kisses on her neck and shoulders. His mouth claimed the straining tip of one full breast, and he spoke around it, rolling it with his tongue between words. "I want to make love to you, Maggie, not just have sex. It . . . was your own . . . idea. . . ."

The hand on her belly slid lower, unerringly finding the warm aching dampness between her legs. He parted, he stroked, and she could have wept with the need building inside her trembling limbs and tight belly. "Please . . ." Her voice was thick with passion, with love. "I've never . . . you're . . . making me . . ."

"What, Maggie?" He slipped one finger inside while he kissed and nibbled his way lower. "What am I making you? What have you never?"

"I've never felt this way before." Her head rolled on the pillow while ecstasy built. "I want you . . . inside me, Chase. I want you so much."

"You'll have me," he promised. His cheek pressed against the curls at the juncture of her thighs just before he covered her with his mouth. His tongue dipped inside and shoved her over the edge and into a wild orgasmic free-fall.

BASKING IN THE AFTERGLOW of his lovemaking, Maggie looked through half-closed eyes into the face of the man with whom she was hopelessly in love.

Chase Britton. Who'd have thought it? Who'd have imagined that after all her bad luck, she'd now cut her own throat—by falling for a man completely out of her league?

He was champagne and she was beer; he was a king and she a serving maid. She chewed on her trembling bottom lip. He was a master of seduction and she was starving for love.

She looked down at their bodies in the tangle of sheets. One of her hands rested on his stomach; one of his hands cupped her breast, the fingers idly toying with her nipple.

Making her want him again, and after that she'd want him again and again and yet again, she had no doubt. As she remembered the way he'd touched her, teased her, inflamed her with hands and mouth and tongue before possessing her the way she longed to be possessed, she turned her head into his chest and groaned. Without thinking, she flicked out her tongue to touch his flat nipple.

He gasped, his entire body stiffening. Encouraged by his response, she rolled over and reached down between them with greedy hands.

"Ahhh . . ." His sigh was languorous. "I wondered what you were thinking, Maggie sweetheart."

"I was thinking—" she began to fondle his increasing erection "—that I would very much like to do—" her other hand joined her first, sliding up and down his hard pulsating flesh "—for you what you did for me."

Chase's voice was a sexy growl. "By all means, be my guest."

He rolled onto his back. She noticed, as she knelt between his thighs, that his hands were fisted into the sheets, as if to keep himself firmly anchored for her pleasure—*their* pleasure.

She bent and took him into her mouth. Her tongue made little swirling explorations and she moved with joyful deliberation, savoring the tastes and texture, the responsiveness of his beautiful body, so supremely male.

For once, he was in her power. She intended to make the most of it.

SHE LAY IN HIS ARMS, looking drowsy and replete and utterly wonderful. The tender curve of her mouth brought a smile of satisfaction to his own. That mouth had brought him incredible pleasure. Perhaps she hadn't shown him any new moves, but she'd introduced him to new feelings....

What was he going to do if she left? Blair would be miserable. To be honest, he wouldn't be too happy, either. He'd misjudged her. She hadn't been coming on to him that first time in Cupid. She'd been trying to defend herself from temptation, and she'd done a good job.

Hell, a woman had the same right as a man to explore the sensual side of her nature, but he was pleased that Maggie had chosen not to—until now. With him.

She sighed and snuggled her cheek against his shoulder. "What time is it?" she murmured, the brush of soft lips making his skin tingle.

"I can't see the clock," he said evasively. If she knew it was nearly five in the morning, she'd leap from his bed, and he wasn't ready to let her go. One more for the road, he rationalized—maybe two if he hurried.

She kissed his throat. "I've got to get out of here before Blair wakes up."

"I suppose," he conceded, but his arms tightened around her. He would keep her as long as he could, both in his bed and in his house.

For his daughter's sake.

For his sake, if he was going to keep the best sex he ever had.

"Maggie?"

"Mmm?"

He took a deep breath. Did he really want to do this? Before he could make a rational choice, he heard himself say, "What the hell. Let's get married."

MAGGIE SAT UP, brushing back her mane of hair with one bent arm. "What did you say?"

"Let's get married."

"*Why?*"

"Hell, isn't it obvious?"

She fought to remain calm. "Not to me, it isn't."

"I don't want you to go," he said.

Her heart skipped a beat. Could he possibly be about to add the only thing that would make this right? God knew she'd like nothing more than to marry him. If he said he loved her, she'd follow him anywhere, give him anything that was hers to give.

But she was damned if she'd be his live-in tutor-cum-sex-toy, no matter how desperately she loved him. "Why?" she asked again.

He was beginning to look decidedly uncomfortable. "Blair needs you," he said, "and . . . so do I."

Her heart felt as if it had been turned to stone. "In your bed, you mean."

"Well, yes. Sure. I wouldn't propose marriage for my daughter's sake alone. Hell, Maggie, what we've started here won't just go away. Everything's changed now." His voice turned intimate, cajoling. "I've got my good points, you said so yourself. For example, I can be a very generous man."

She knew that. He could be generous indeed in a sexual sense; emotionally he'd destroy her. He reached out to caress her knee and she slapped his hand away. "Don't!"

"Maggie, you'll have everything you ever wanted. Blair will be happy, I'll be happy, you'll be—"

"Gone."

He curled his hand around her ankle as if to hold her there. "Didn't you hear me? I'm offering marriage."

"Well, whoop-de-do! It feels like a slap in the face."

"Wait a minute." He shook his head, frowning. "Since when is a marriage proposal considered an insult?"

"When the wrong reasons are behind it." She stared at him, realizing he had no idea why she was upset. "Do you love me, Chase?"

He sucked in a breath. "I . . . like you. A lot actually. Probably as much as I've ever cared for any woman. Maybe as much as it's in me to care."

She just looked at him.

That seemed to give him new hope. "So let's get married," he said more confidently. "We can tell Blair at breakfast. It'll make all the difference to her."

Maggie pushed herself to the edge of the bed and stood up, snatching up and pulling on the clothing they'd discarded in such haste last night.

"Dammit, Maggie, will you marry me or not?"

She turned back toward the bed and looked at him with all the scorn she could summon; tears and regrets and despair would come later. "No! Is that plain enough for you? No! When I get married again—" she laughed bitterly "—*if* I get married again, it'll be for the same reason I got married the first time—love. I won't betray what's in here—" she brought a clenched fist to her breast "—for good sex."

"*Good* sex?"

"Great sex—so what? It's not enough! You don't love me and never pretended you did, so don't insult me now."

He folded his long legs and leaned forward with his elbows on his knees. "Sweetheart, you don't love me, either, so what are you bitching about?"

She stopped with her hand on the doorknob. "You don't really know that, do you," she reminded him softly. "You never bothered to ask."

She opened the door.

"But what'll I tell Blair?" he demanded. "Damn, what a mess."

"Tell her I've gone back home where I belong. She can pass any test the school district wants to throw at her and always could. Tell her . . . I love her and I'm sorry." She took the first step out of his life. "You can mail me my check."

Maggie walked out, closing the door very carefully and softly behind her.

She longed to slam it off its hinges, but there were a lot of things she longed for that she could no longer afford.

CHASE, HUNKERED OVER his fifth cup of coffee, heard footsteps and looked up without enthusiasm. Maggie had gone, leaving him alone to face the wild child who was his daughter.

Blair walked into the kitchen and looked around cautiously. He waited for her to ask about Maggie.

Instead, she said, "Good morning, Father."

Chase bit back a groan. Now what was she up to? "Good morning, Daughter," he responded dryly. He shoved a cereal box toward her. "Care for another of my gourmet breakfasts?"

"My, my, aren't we funny this morning."

Walking to the cabinet, she withdrew her favorite cereal. It was full of sugar and artificial color and artificial flavor and other crap that he knew wasn't good for her. Maggie had *tsk-tsked* when he'd brought it into the house, but he was weak where Blair was concerned. He watched her pour the hideous stuff into her bowl, then begin eating it by dry handfuls.

"Blair," he began in a warning tone, "you know that stuff'll rot your innards. At least add milk."

She looked him right in the eye and stuffed in another mouthful. "Thanks for letting me sleep late this morning," she said, "even if I wasn't sleeping."

It didn't sound like thanks, but he said, "You're welcome," just the same.

"You look rotten," she said. The comment appeared to give her pleasure.

"Yeah, and that's the good news."

Her smile was innocent, her voice insincere. "I'm sorry about yesterday."

Where was this going? Chase frowned, completely adrift. How the hell was he supposed to figure out the twelve-year-old female mind—or any female mind? He, who prided himself on sensitivity and good manners, felt completely adrift. "Are you?" he asked finally.

"Oh, sure." She poured milk into her bowl as if to appease him. "It was all a misunderstanding. I don't really care who you marry. You do want to get married again someday, don't you?"

"Not in this lifetime," he said. "Why are you so hot to get me married all of a sudden?"

"I don't know," she said vaguely. "I think you maybe need, like, a hobby."

"A hobby!" He stifled a curse. His daughter was nuts.

"I thought if you married Maggie, you'd forget about me and let me go to Switzerland."

"You are not going to Switzerland." He had to force the words past clenched teeth.

"But—" she looked suddenly very young and very confused "—Maggie said—"

"It doesn't matter what Maggie said. She's gone." He stood, braced his palms on the breakfast bar and leaned forward. "I don't want to hear another word about Switzerland or Maggie or anything else you dream up to make my life miserable. You catch my drift? From now on, things around here are going to be different."

Blair looked stricken; all the color washed out of her cheeks. "Maggie's gone?"

"That's right. She said to tell you—"

"*How could you!* What did you do to her? You're a horrible, awful, rotten . . ." She jumped to her feet, her body rigid.

"Stop it, Blair. I didn't do anything to Maggie." Nothing she didn't *want* done. "It was her decision. I couldn't very well hold her captive, now could I."

"Why not?" Blair shot back. "That's what you're doing to me." She took several steps back, out of his reach.

"Blair—"

"Leave me alone! Just leave me alone!"

It was beginning to look as if the only way she knew to leave a room was in a rage. Chase started after her but then stopped. What was he going to say to her? He wouldn't let her go to school abroad and couldn't promise to get Maggie back. He couldn't promise anything, except that he would do his duty even if it killed them both.

"MAMA, MAMA, it's me, Blair. Oh, Mama—"

"Blair! What a surprise. Is something wrong?"

Blair shifted the telephone to a more comfortable position. "Everything's wrong, Mama. I hate him!"

"Who, your father? Don't be silly. Uh . . . this isn't a very good time. I'm sure everything will be just fine if you'll try—"

"I do try! Mama, let me come back to live with you, please? I think he's mad enough at me to let me go now. I know he forced—"

"Now, Blair, you're just upset. Your father's not *that* bad."

"But you always said—"

"What did I say? Just that he was a real pain in the— Oh, I don't have time for this, really I don't. I have a doctor's appointment in twenty minutes."

"You're sick? Oh, Mama, what's wrong?" Blair's heart threatened to burst with anxiety.

"I'm not sick, honey. I'm . . . pregnant."

"P-pregnant?" The girl's voice rose. "You're going to have a baby?"

"Yes. Mark and I are very happy about it. I hope you're happy for us."

"But . . ." Horrible possibilities flooded Blair's reeling mind. Her mother would have another baby to love. She'd forget she already had a daughter.

"Make up with your father, Blair. He's not an ogre."

"But you said— Mama, I know he forced you to make me live with him, but now I think he's sorry he did. I can help you, Mama. I'll take care of the baby for you. I'll be good. I won't cause any more trouble with Mark, I promise." Blair's teeth chattered so hard she had to stop talking.

"It's not that simple. I can't just come and get you. I signed a paper—"

"A paper?"

"That's the only way he'd take you. Oh, I don't mean that the way it sounds, sweetheart, but you know how you got on Mark's nerves. I did it for you. You were better off in Aspen. I never thought of anything except your good, you know that."

"Daddy didn't want me, either?"

"Of course he wanted you," her mother said. "Now quit whining and act your age. You could do worse than grow up in Aspen with a rich daddy and all the advantages. I did you a favor."

Not as big a favor as you did for yourself, Blair thought numbly, standing there with the dial tone in her ear. She looked up at the ceiling of her room, wondering what she would do now.

"LIBBY, YOU'VE GOT to help me!"

"Good grief, Blair, what's wrong? You sound awful."

"I am. You don't know—"

"Are you crying? Oh, Blair, did he *hit* you?"

"Almost. I thought he was going to. Libby, he fired Maggie."

"Oh, no!"

"Yes. She was my only friend. He fired her because I love her, and I hate him for it."

"You already hated him. Didn't you?"

"I called my mother."

"Oh, Blair! Are you going to live with her? I'll miss you so much if you do."

"She...she's too busy. But I can't stay with this crazy man another minute. That's where you come in, Libby. Here's what I need you to do—and don't let me down! If you do, I think I might . . . kill myself!"

"Don't talk like that. Just tell me what you want me to do . . ."

11

THE FIRST WORDS out of Betsy's mouth were, "Something's wrong."

"Who gave you the clue, Dick Tracy?" Maggie's attempt at humor fell flat.

"I guess it would be too much to hope you're home simply because your work is finished and the Brittons are ready to live happily ever after."

"It's finished, all right, but the end result remains in serious doubt." Maggie tugged her suitcase out of the back seat of her car and started for the house, Betsy falling into step. "I'm finished, too. God, Betts, I've made such a mess of everything."

"I'm sure it's not as bad as it seems, whatever you're talking about." Betsy slipped her arm around her sister-in-law's waist. "You are going to tell me everything, aren't you?"

Maggie sighed. "I have to talk to somebody," she said slowly. "If you're willing to listen ..."

"I'm even willing to help if I can."

"Okay, as soon as I check in with Grandma we'll talk. And, Betsy—" Maggie halted at the front door "—thank you."

Betsy responded with a sweet smile and a big hug.

It was good to be home.

THE TWO WOMEN sat on the front steps, glasses of iced tea beside them. For a few moments they remained silent, looking out at the neat outbuildings and corrals of the Straight Arrow Ranch. After a while, Betsy glanced at Maggie cautiously.

"You slept with him, didn't you."

Maggie groaned. "Elizabeth Cameron, I can't believe you'd say such a thing."

"Why not? I can believe you'd *do* such a thing." Betsy smiled. "What are you so upset about? You're of age, you're eligible. You deserve a little pleasure, just like everybody else." Her blue eyes revealed sympathy. "Am I safe in assuming it *was* a pleasure?"

Maggie groaned and buried her face in her hands. "Yes. Oh, yes. But . . . how did you guess?"

"There's something different about you. It's like some of your hard edges have been smoothed away. Does that make sense? You're softer, more . . ."

"Vulnerable." Maggie lifted her head. "I still haven't come to terms with it in my own mind, Betsy."

"You mean you're not sure how you feel about him now?"

"That's not it at all. I know exactly how I feel about him. I just don't know what good it's going to do me— Oh, who am I kidding? It's not going to do me *any* good. It just makes me even more aware of what I'm missing."

"No chance for the two of you, then?"

"None whatsoever. He doesn't love me, Betts. I'm not even sure he likes me. He—"

The screen door opened and Granny stuck her head through. "Land's sakes, here you girls are. You got a phone call, Maggie."

Her heart leapt. "Who is it?"

"It's Chase." She must have seen the anger flare on her granddaughter's face, because she said, "Now don't get up on your high horse. His—"

"I've got nothing to say to Chase Britton, now or ever."

"You sure as shootin' do. His little girl's disappeared, and he's goin' out of his mind with worry. You get your fanny in here and *talk* to the man."

"SHE'S THERE with you, isn't she?" Chase despised the raw fear in his voice but couldn't control it. "Or at least, you must know where she is."

"No, of course not. Don't you think I'd have called?"

His silence spoke volumes.

"You misjudge me, Chase." Maggie sounded unutterably sad.

"Then you haven't heard from her at all?"

"No, I swear it." She paused. "Did anything else happen after I left?"

"You could say that." He gave a harsh bark of laughter. "I told her you were gone and Switzerland was out. She didn't take it well."

"I'm sorry. I wish I could've said goodbye to her, but I was afraid that would make it even harder."

"For whom? Her, me . . . or you?"

He'd gone too far; he knew it when she didn't answer for an interminable length of time. Then she said, very softly, "If you believe that, Chase, then we have nothing more to say to each other."

He stood there before a dead telephone, trying to cope with this, his worst nightmare. Despite his very best efforts, he'd been unable to win the affection or trust of his child. Blair preferred Maggie to him, and the worst part of it was, he didn't blame her.

Making matters worse, he'd burned his bridges with Maggie. Proposing had been the right thing to do, done for all the wrong reasons. He didn't want to marry Maggie for Blair's sake.

He wanted to marry Maggie for his own sake because . . .

He loved her. He loved every damned thing about her, from her tart tongue to her prickly nature to her intuitive understanding of his daughter's heart. He loved Maggie's frowns because they made her smiles all the more precious. Last but never least, he loved to love her . . .

Not just her body, which seemed made especially for him with its ability to give and take pleasure, but the woman: Margaret Cameron Colby. But he'd screwed up big-time and doubted she'd ever believe him now. In the space of a few hours, Chase Britton, he of the charmed life, had lost the two females who meant the most to him in all the world.

At that moment, life really sucked—but he'd be damned if he'd curl up and die.

A DUSTY LITTLE JEEP pulled into the ranch yard, and Blair Britton jumped out. Waving to the driver, she waited until he'd yanked the vehicle into a U-turn and hauled out of there before turning toward the house.

Maggie came running down the steps. "Blair! Thank God!" She wrapped her arms around the girl, lifting her off her feet. "We were so worried!"

"You mean he already knows I'm gone?" Blair's mouth curved down petulantly. "I guess he knew I'd come here."

"It was an easy guess, sweetie." Maggie steered Blair toward the house. "Was that Libby's brother driving the Jeep?"

"Please don't tell," Blair begged. "I blackmailed him into it. If anybody finds out, he's in megatrouble. I had to do it, though—either that or hitchhike."

"Never ever hitchhike. It's incredibly dangerous." Maggie shuddered. "I'm just grateful you're here and you're safe. As soon as I call your father, we'll have a nice long—"

"No! Please don't call him!"

"But I have to." Maggie took both of Blair's hands and drew her down on the front steps. "Honey, he's worried sick."

"He's just a big fake." She blinked furiously at the tears trembling on her lashes. "I know the truth now. He never wanted me, not even to make Mama suffer. He only took me because he had to, because she . . ."

With a strangled cry, she collapsed into Maggie's comforting embrace. Poor kid, Maggie thought, her own eyes growing moist. Blair must have spoken to her mother. Damn the woman! Maggie's arms tightened protectively around the weeping girl. How were they ever going to make this right?

INSIDE THE HOUSE, Betsy was already talking to Chase. "Yes, she's here. We wanted you to know right away... She just got here, Chase. Calm down. Some kid in a Jeep dropped her off and then split. She's out front with Maggie . . . Well, yes, they're both crying actually.

"I don't *know* what the problem— Chase! We'll take care of her—you don't need to worry about that. But if you'd like a friendly little piece of advice . . . I know you're hurting, but listen to me. Give us a few days to calm her down, why don't you. I'll tell her you called, that you're very relieved she's safe. We'll do our best to present your side of it . . . Yes, Maggie, too, you big bonehead . . .

"Okay, I'll have Maggie call you later tonight, after we know more. But in the meantime . . . That's right, sit tight. And, Chase . . . it'll work out. Trust me on this."

Betsy hung up the telephone and sighed, praying that she hadn't lied to one of her oldest and dearest friends.

BLAIR COULDN'T HAVE BEEN sweeter or more docile than she was to the Camerons. Maggie knew the girl was trying to ingratiate herself so they'd take her side against her father, but couldn't condemn her for it.

Instead, she condemned herself. The more Blair clung to her, the guiltier she felt. Who, more than she, knew to what lengths Chase would go for his child?

He'd even tie himself in marriage to a woman he didn't love.

Maggie had come home to put that humiliation behind her, but Blair's presence made it impossible. Even with her heart in shards, Maggie knew she must rise to defend Chase against his daughter's defamations.

Which had become much more subtle. Apparently the girl realized she couldn't simply throw wild accusations around and expect to gain the sympathies of the Camerons, so she muted her complaints.

At dinner that first evening, to Granny's delight, she devoured chicken-fried steak as if it were going out of style. "This is really good," she said, wiping her mouth with her napkin. "My father won't let me eat stuff like this."

Granny reared back in her chair. "Why not? This is good wholesome food."

"He says fried stuff's bad for you."

"Balderdash!"

Maggie sighed. This was an ongoing source of friction in the Cameron household, and Blair had stumbled right into the middle it. Granny, who did most of the cooking, wanted to cook the way she always had, while Julie and Betsy fought a constant battle against grease and cholesterol. Granny's chicken-fried steak was delicious, but a steady diet of it would clog anybody's arteries.

Julie leaned forward. "Now, Granny, her father's right. She shouldn't be eating fried foods. Neither should the rest of us."

"Once in a while won't hurt anybody," Granny grumped.

"I don't think I've had two hamburgers since I moved to Aspen," Blair said self-righteously. "And french fries, forget it."

Lisa Marie had been listening to the exchange, her curly head rotating between speakers. "Joey doesn't like french fries," she announced.

"I do too!" Joey gave her chair a shove with his shoulder. He was almost a year older than his stepsister and not about to let her speak for him.

"Then why," Lisa Marie inquired serenely, "do you throw them at me, instead of eating them?"

"Because!" Joey looked at Blair with interest. "Does your dad make you eat junk like broccoli?"

"I love broccoli," Lisa Marie declared.

"I hate it!" Joey snapped back.

"I love . . . I love carrots."

"Barf!"

"Joey!" Betsy, spooning mashed potatoes and peas into two-year-old Catherine, frowned at the boy. "We do not say 'barf' at the dinner table."

"Sorry, Mom. I forgot."

Joey hunched his shoulders, properly chastened. Maggie knew he really was sorry. The boy adored his stepmother and would do anything to please her.

Betsy smiled and gave Joey a quick hug, which wasn't lost on Blair. She looked down quickly at her empty plate.

It wasn't lost on Lisa Marie, either. "Poor Blair, doesn't your mama ever hug you?" the little girl asked.

Blair looked up with a stricken expression. "My mother lives...someplace else. I don't see her a-anymore."

Lisa Marie's face revealed melting compassion. "Do you miss her?"

Betsy shushed her daughter. "Lisa, don't ask such personal questions."

"But I want to know," Lisa Marie said reasonably. "I remember your daddy, Blair. Doesn't *he* ever hug you? My daddy hugs me, because I make him. I put my arms around him and squeeze real hard, and he always says—" she launched into a fair imitation of Ben's drawl "—'Betsy, that girl's gonna grow up to be an Amazon.'" She giggled. "But he hugs me back!"

Everybody laughed except Blair. Maggie reached beneath the table to pat the girl's hand in a gesture of support. Blair gave her a small grateful smile.

Joey put down his fork with a bang. "Who wants to be an old Amazon, anyway. I'm gonna be a cowboy. What's for dessert?"

"Ice cream," Granny said. She turned her twinkling gray eyes on Blair. "I bet your daddy lets you eat ice cream."

"I don't like ice cream." Blair placed her napkin on the table and stood. "Dinner was delicious. Please excuse me."

Maggie followed the girl's headlong rush from the table. Behind them, Lisa Marie called out, "Not dinner, Blair. This was supper."

"Shush!" That was Betsy's whisper. "It doesn't matter what you call it."

And Joey's delighted cackle of laughter. "Let's call it breakfast, Lisa."

"Or sup-fast, or din-fast."

"Or break-lunch. Hey, *brunch* is a real word!"

"Nah, you made it up."

"Will you kids pipe down?" said Ben. "Granny, I'll take a man-size dish of that ice cream . . ."

Life in the Cameron household, Maggie thought wryly as she hurried upstairs. Blair and her father usually ate in wary silence, made worse by frequent flare-ups. Maggie felt sorry for both of them.

She found Blair lying crosswise on one of the twin beds staring dry-eyed at the ceiling. "Lisa Marie and Joey and Cat are lucky kids," she said in a flat voice.

"They've had their problems." Maggie sat down on the side of the bed. "Did you know that Joey's real mother and Lisa's real father are dead?"

"Really?" Blair frowned, digesting this new information. "What about Cat?"

"She's Ben and Betsy's."

"You sure can't tell any difference." Blair squeezed her eyes shut. "They're still lucky. They have parents who love them."

"So do you, sweetheart." Maggie rested a hand on the girl's shoulder, squeezing lightly. "And you love them, if you'll just be honest."

"No, I don't. I hate them—both of them. My mother's no better than my father. They're sorry they ever had me."

"That's not true. I don't know your mother, but I can tell you that your father loves you and would do anything to—"

"Anything? Ha! He won't let me go away to school."

"That's because he wants you near him," Maggie said patiently for perhaps the hundredth time. "What else would make you happy, Blair? If it's within his power . . ."

"There is something." Blair's expression turned almost sly, and she lowered her eyelids as if to conceal her thoughts.

Maggie felt a leap of hope. Maybe she'd still be able to find a way to reconcile father and daughter. "Tell me."

Blair sat up on the bed and scooted around, messing up the blue bedspread in the process. Her eyes had taken on a half-wild glow and she cried, "I want to stay here forever! I love you, Maggie! You can be my mother. Please say you will."

And she threw her frantic body into Maggie's arms and hung on for dear life.

"OH, DEAR," Julie said. "So what did you tell her?"

"That it was impossible. And she said, 'But I'd still live close to him—if that's what he really wants.'"

Maggie reached for another dish, towel at the ready. Her hand trembled so badly she had to get a better grip before she lifted the bowl.

Julie swished a skillet through the tub of rinse water before placing it in the draining rack. From the living room, they heard the murmur of Betsy's voice as she read to the children from one of the *Little House* books Lisa Marie loved so much. The girl had heard them innumerable times and adored them; Joey had heard them innumerable times and declared them boring, but kept listening in case later editions contained a little murder and mayhem.

Tonight, Blair listened, too. Maggie had left the girl sitting on the floor with Cat nestled on her lap. Maggie didn't believe she'd ever seen Chase's daughter so happy and relaxed. Even Grandma enjoyed the nightly read-a-thons, although Ben had muttered something about "fairy tales" and gone off to his office to work on the books.

Julie gave her sister a compassionate glance. "So, what did you tell her?"

"That it was impossible for her to stay more than a few days, and that her father was being extremely generous to allow even that. She said, 'Ha! What does he care? If he loved me he'd already be here to take me home. This just proves . . .' Well, you get the idea. And I told her Betsy had talked him into letting her stay for a few days until she felt better, and she smiled and said she loved Betsy, too. And you and Ben and Granny and... Damn, Julie, I thought she was going to name every living critter on the Straight Arrow."

"Poor Maggie."

"Poor Blair. Poor Chase."

"No, poor *Maggie*. I get the feeling there's not much you'd like better than being that girl's mother—unless it's being her father's wife."

"Grow up, Julie." Maggie slammed down a pan so hard the cabinet vibrated. "What would a man like Chase Britton want with a country mouse like me? He's no fan of marriage, anyway—he'll probably never get married again. If he does, it won't be to the likes of me, so cut it out."

Julie stared at her sister throughout that impassioned outburst. "If that's how you feel, maybe you should call Chase and tell him to come get her right away. Cut your losses, so to speak."

"No." Maggie's lips tightened. "I need—Blair needs a little more time." Although all the time in the world might not be enough to change the girl's mind.

Julie emptied her tub of soapy water into the sink. "I don't know, Maggie. The longer she stays, the harder it'll be on you, and the harder it may be to get her to go back. But if you want her here, I guess you can suggest it to him."

"I can't talk to him now. You do it ... okay?"

"But—"

"Please. I mean it, I simply can't talk to the man."

"Oh, all right. But I don't feel good about this. I think you've got Chase all wrong. But if you've got a problem with him, you should try to work it out for Blair's sake."

"Who says I ever have to see Chase Britton again?" Maggie hadn't even thought of that possibility until she said it, but immediately knew it to be true. When he came for his daughter, Maggie could be conveniently away somewhere. Anywhere.

Maggie tossed her damp dish towel on the counter. "You finish," she said in a strangled voice. "I've got to . . ."

Get used to living with this big hole in my heart.

OVER THE NEXT several days, Maggie talked to Blair until, in Granny's vernacular, she was blue in the face. Carefully and in great detail, she explained to the girl that her father wouldn't arrive momentarily to drag her away, but that under no circumstances would he allow her to go to school abroad.

"Give him a chance," Maggie pleaded again and again. "He loves you. Give *yourself* a chance to love him back."

She thought she was making at least a little headway. For one thing, the girl was much calmer. She entered into the life of the family with enthusiasm, accepting her share of chores without protest, playing with the younger children, cheerfully running errands for Granny, even helping Ben every chance she got. She willingly performed every task he gave her, from shov-

eling manure to helping shoo runaway calves back into
the corral.

"You said I'd make a good hand," she reminded him
shyly the third afternoon of her stay, after the last of the
dogies had been rounded up.

"I did say that, didn't I." Ben grinned, looking for all
the world like the Marlboro man, Maggie thought.
She'd been lending a hand, too.

"Well?" Blair nudged. "How'm I doin'?"

Ben threw back his head and laughed. "Fair," he allowed, very tongue in cheek. "Just fair. When you get
a 'good' outta me, you'll know you earned it."

Blair was happier with Ben's "fair" than she'd been
with her father's raves, Maggie realized.

"I'll earn it," the girl said with a determination that
made her voice quiver. "Thanks, Mr. Cameron.
Thanks a lot."

Later Ben drew Maggie aside. "That girl's gettin' way
too attached to all of us," he warned. "You know I've
never cared a whole hell of a lot for Chase Britton, but
I don't want to get between any man and what's his, just
like I'd let no man get between me and what's mine."

Or what you want to be yours, Maggie thought, remembering how possessive her brother had been during his courtship of Betsy. "Ben, there was never
anything between Chase and Betsy," she said. "The
chance that there was is all you've got against him, and
you know it."

Ben's gray eyes narrowed. "I don't know it, Maggie. I got a hunch he hasn't been too straight where *you're* concerned."

"You're wrong. He never deceived me, didn't even try to." Saying it, she knew it was true. "Any . . . problems are of my own making. Live and learn, Ben."

"If we're lucky. I was. I hope you end up lucky, too."

"Not much chance of that, but there's still time for Blair. We've got to get her and her father back together again. We've *got* to."

He nodded slowly. "You're right about that."

Satisfied, Maggie watched her brother disappear into the barn. Maybe between the bunch of them, they'd be able to convince Blair that her father's stance was more than pure stubbornness.

CHASE GOT THE CALL at the restaurant, where he'd spent practically all his time since Maggie and Blair had left. Not that work really took his mind off his problems, but it did help the days pass while he tried to figure out what the hell to do next.

When his secretary told him Ben Cameron was on the line, Chase groaned. As if he hadn't been kicked enough lately. Then a horrible thought occurred to him: what if something was wrong with Blair?

He grabbed the telephone. "Cameron? What's wrong? Is Blair—?"

"She's fine. Take it easy."

"Then what . . . ?"

"You better come get her."

Chase frowned. "But Betsy said I ought to leave her there for a while. Of course, if she's in your way..."

"Hell, she's not in anybody's way." The rancher sounded disgusted. "We like her. She pitches in, does her share."

"You're talking about Blair Britton, my daughter?"

"That's the one."

"Then what's the problem? If she wants to come home, all she has to do is pick up the phone. So could Betsy or—" he swallowed "—Maggie. Why'd they ask you to do it?"

"They didn't ask me," Ben responded with exaggerated patience. "I'm doin' this on my own hook. Blair's gettin' way too attached to us. Hell, she hangs on to Maggie like she was her mother, and it's tearin' Maggie up. There's nothin' to be gained by more time, as I see it. You two got to make peace now or you never will."

"Damn!" Chase realized he was no closer to knowing how to handle his runaway daughter now than when she'd first taken off. "You got any suggestions on how I can do that?" Hell, now he was asking for advice from Ben Cameron.

"The way I see it, you got two choices," Ben drawled. "You can lay down the law and drag her back home by the hair of her head—"

Chase flinched. Was this guy for real?

"—or you can give her what the hell it is she's so damned determined to have and live with the consequences. It's up to you, but I'd say it was time to do something, even if you do it wrong."

Unfortunately, Chase thought, that was all too true.

12

"I'M COMING to get you," Chase told his daughter. "Be ready."

"No! I won't go back and you can't make me!"

He clutched the receiver so hard his knuckles whitened. "I'm not asking you, Blair, I'm telling you. You can't live with the Camerons forever."

"Why not? At least they like me. We *do* things here, not just hang around a stupid old house and a stupid old restaurant."

"You and I can do things. We can—"

"I mean *real* things like riding horses and chasing cows—stuff like that. Stuff you don't know anything about," she added scornfully. "And Granny fries stuff and I eat it and I haven't dropped dead, so there."

"Blair, you're—"

"I'm not going back with you, not ever! If you really loved me, you'd've come after me right away, not waited a week. Now I don't care if I never see you again. In fact, I hope I don't."

She threw down the phone; he heard her sobs fade away and then Maggie said, "Please, Chase, she's not ready. Don't—"

He hung up. Hearing her voice was more than he could handle.

Hearing *his* voice didn't do Maggie a lot of good, either. He was in pain and she was responsible. If she hadn't gotten involved in the first place, they'd all be better off.

The telephone rang again. Maggie, hand still resting on the receiver, jumped a mile. Grabbing it up, she cried, "Thank heaven you called back! You'd be making an awful mistake—"

"Whoa, there, Maggie, I think you gotcher wires crossed."

That voice did not belong to Chase; she didn't know who it belonged to, but definitely not Chase. "Omigosh," she said faintly. "I'm sorry. Who've I got here?"

"It's just me, ol' Marshal Dwight." Dwight Deakins gave a nervous laugh. "You expectin' someone else? I can call back later if—"

"No, no, forgive me. I'd just hung up on another call and thought..." What difference did it make what she'd thought? Chase had hung up on *her*. He couldn't even stand to hear her voice. She pulled herself together. "What can I do for you, Dwight? If you're calling Ben, I'm afraid he's not here."

"I'm callin' *you*, Maggie. Heard you was back in town. So how'd Aspen treat you?"

"Well," she said noncommittally, "you know Aspen."

He laughed. "Sure do. It's a little too rich for my blood, though. I like it right here in good old Cupid."

"So do I, Dwight. So do I." *Or will, as soon as I can cut all ties to the Brittons.* "Uh...I think I hear one of the kids calling me. Was there something else?"

"Now you mention it, I been thinkin'... But you probably wouldn't want to grab a bite at the Hideout with me one of these days or nights... would you?"

He sounded so doggedly hopeful that it shamed her. Dwight obviously wasn't used to life as a bachelor. Maggie figured she was probably the first woman he'd worked up his courage to ask out since his wife had left him.

Maggie should accept. Dwight was a good ol' boy, and she'd known him her entire life. He was free, she was free.

In her dreams. But if she was ever to get over Chase Britton, there was no time like the present to begin. She opened her mouth to accept, but all that came out was a slightly embarrassed squeak.

Dwight took it as a turndown. "Okay, I understand, Maggie. A young chicken like yourself, why would you want to go out with an old rooster like me?"

"It's not like that, Dwight," she said miserably.

"Then you're saying yes?" Jubilation colored his tone. "That's great!"

Sure, why not? Why shouldn't she go out on a friendly little date, no strings attached?

Because she couldn't. It wouldn't be fair when her heart was otherwise engaged. "Would you settle for a cup of coffee one of these days at the Rusty Spur?" She tried to sound casual and upbeat.

"Oh. Oh, sure thing."

He sounded so disappointed she cringed. "I'm really sorry," she murmured. "I've been so busy this summer, and I've got so much to do before school starts this fall.... You understand."

"Yeah, Maggie." He sighed. "I sure do understand."

She hung up, convinced she'd made a mistake. She had to get on with her life.

Obviously it wasn't going to be easy. After Chase, she had no way to go but down.

SEVERAL HOURS LATER, Maggie opened the front door to discover Chase standing on the porch, hat in hand. "What are *you* doing here?" she cried. Without waiting for an answer, she tried to slam the door in his face.

Somehow he managed to wedge a toe in crosswise. A *boot* toe? Surprise made her relax her grip on the door, and it swung open enough to give her a good look at him. Major mistake, since he looked the same only better.

He was dressed like a cowboy in soft worn jeans that caressed those long sleekly muscled legs. His faded chambray work shirt molded his wide shoulders beautifully, and he'd taken a few rolls in the long sleeves, baring powerful forearms.

And damned if that wasn't a Montana peak on his Stetson—a deep crease down the front of the tall crown to funnel off rainwater.

She wondered where he'd come up with such an outfit, but it sure didn't look bad—especially the way those jeans fit every bulge and angle.

"You through looking?" he asked. His eyes were tired, his expression without humor or cheer.

She started. "Yes. So, what are you doing here, Chase? I thought you understood—"

"I came to get my daughter, just like I said I would. Where is she?" He peered beyond Maggie into the living room. Which was empty.

"She's down at the corrals with Ben and the kids, but..."

He spun around and took off down the porch steps in twos, his strides long and determined. She hurried to catch up with him, then grabbed at his arm.

Which was another mistake. Touching him sent a shock up her arm that made it tingle all the way to the shoulder. But she accomplished her purpose, for he whirled to confront her, his eyes hooded.

"What's your problem, Maggie? I had to come get her sooner or later."

"Later would be better. We've all been working on her, Chase. I think she's about to come around, but..."

"'But,' my foot. She's just a kid, and I've let her call my bluff too often. It's time she learned who's boss." He started walking again.

Maggie hurried along beside him, but this time didn't risk touching him. "Don't be too hard on her—please? I think she spoke to her mother, which may have set this whole thing in motion."

"Nikki." He spat the name with disgust. "I thought of that, but she denied it. I'll bet she told Blair—" He clamped off the words.

"Told her what?"

"Nikki's pregnant."

"Oh, no! Poor Blair already felt abandoned. That must have been a devastating blow to her."

"Water under the bridge. My mind is made up."

Maggie's stomach clenched painfully. "What are you going to do?"

"I'm not about to run my plans past you for approval," he said acidly. "It's really none of your business anymore, is it."

They reached the corral just as Ben led a pony out into the sunshine. All three kids scampered around, getting in his and the animal's way. Ben feigned anger. "You kids watch out. Ol' Poco here would just as soon step on you as look at you."

"No, he wouldn't, Daddy," Lisa Marie disagreed calmly. "Old Dobbin might, but not Poco." She was the first to spot Chase, and she waved. "Look, it's Blair's daddy. Hi, Mr. Britton! Wanna go riding with us?"

Blair's face went white, and she took a step back, looking around wildly as if seeking an escape route. Apparently finding none, she faced her father across the corral. "He won't go riding with us," she said scornfully, answering Lisa Marie's question while throwing out a fresh challenge to her father. "He's a *dude*."

Such a dirty word when it fell from her lips. A spark of anger flared in her father's hazel eyes.

"A dude, am I?" Chase leapt lightly onto the corral logs and threw his legs over the top, dropping to the ground inside with agile grace. "Sweetheart, there's a helluva lot you don't know about your old dad."

Blair looked momentarily confused; then her shoulders squared. "I know that wearing cowboy clothes won't make you a cowboy." She appealed to Ben. "That's right, isn't it, Mr. Cameron? That's what you said." Her vindictive glance toward her father added, *So there!*

Ben shoved his battered hat to the back of his head, his eyes sparkling. "That's what I said, little girl. But I should've added that you can't judge a book by its cover."

"I've never seen him rope a calf or ride a horse," she argued. "I've never seen him do anything except criticize the wine and send stuff back to the chef."

"That does it," Chase grated. "Saddle up that Dobbin horse."

Maggie, standing on the bottom rung of the corral fence with her arms resting on the top, cried out in alarm. "Don't be ridiculous, Chase. You have nothing to prove."

Slowly he turned. "Don't I?" he asked softly.

Ben took command. "Maggie, get these kids and that pony outta here."

"You can't be a party to this, Ben!"

His brows rose. "Hell I can't. A man's gotta do what a man's gotta do. I get the feeling that for this man it's way *over*due." He disappeared into the dark interior of the barn.

Chase opened the corral gate and waved kids and pony through. Joey and Lisa Marie looked interested, while Blair merely looked defensive.

"Don't blame me if you fall on your butt," she said unpleasantly.

For a long moment, her defiant gaze met her father's weary one. Then he nodded abruptly. "I don't blame you for anything," he said. "None of this is your fault. It's mine and your mother's. But one way or the other, we've got to get past it and go on."

Together or separately, Maggie realized with a sudden chill. "Chase . . ." She started forward.

He swung the corral gate closed with a bang, effectively shutting her out. "Save your breath, Maggie."

"But you don't understand." She clung to the gate. "Dobbin is one mean animal. You don't know what you're doing. You could be seriously hurt. Killed, even." She shivered. "Don't do this, please."

He turned his back on her. She scrambled to the top rail of the corral, her entire body knotted with concern.

Blair climbed up, too. "Don't worry," the girl said scornfully. "He won't do it."

Maggie gave Blair an exasperated glance. "Of course he's going to do it. He couldn't very well back down now, even if he wanted to."

Blair looked uncertain. "Could he really get hurt?"

"Yes!" Maggie gentled her tone. "Horses can be dangerous under the best of circumstances. Put an inexperienced rider and a bad horse together, and anything can happen."

"B-but—" Blair's mouth trembled "—if he gets hurt, what'll happen to me? Mama won't let me live with her and— Oh!" She clamped one hand over her mouth, her eyes round as doughnuts.

Maggie put an arm over the girl's hunched shoulders. "Is that the only thing you're worried about?" she asked gently. "Couldn't it be that you really do love your father and don't want to see him get hurt?"

"No!" Quick tears started in Blair's hazel eyes. "M-maybe I would love him if he really loved me. But he doesn't, Maggie. I know he doesn't."

Maggie smoothed the hair away from Blair's forehead. "Sweetheart, if he didn't love you, he'd send you to Switzerland in a heartbeat. But, instead, he's run himself ragged trying to win your love and your respect. I have a feeling this stunt . . ."

She looked out into the center of the corral, where Ben had tied Dobbin to the snubbing post. The big horse trembled in anticipation, whites of his eyes showing balefully while Ben saddled him up. "This is one last stab at winning you over."

Blair shook her head. "No way."

Betsy with Cat in her arms, and Granny with a dish towel flapping, arrived at a run. Granny wiped her hands on the towel before tossing it over one shoulder. "What in tarnation are them men up to?" she demanded. "My stars, is Ben about to put Blair's daddy up on ol' Dobbin?"

Maggie leaned down, speaking urgently. "Can you stop them, Granny? Chase could get killed!"

Granny reared back. "Have a little faith, Maggie. I got a feelin' the man knows what—"

"Ride 'em, cowboy!" Ben released his hold on Dobbin's ears and leapt away.

THE FIRST JUMP caught Chase by surprise, but he found his balance before Dobbin came down in a stiff-legged landing that jarred his rider's teeth but didn't dislodge him. Ducking his head, the horse started pitching in earnest, traveling across the corral in rough little crow hops.

It'd been a long time since Chase had straddled a bucking bronc. Dobbin was a sincere if untalented bucker. Any rider surviving that first hop shouldn't have too much to worry about.

Unless he let himself be distracted by an audience. Blair and Maggie flashed past, and Chase had a quick impression of his daughter's pale face and Maggie's astonished expression. She'd had no idea. Her brother had, though. Chase found himself thinking he might have more in common with Ben Cameron than either of them had imagined.

"Keep his head up!" Ben hollered.

Chase glimpsed a hat fanned against the top rail and recognized the other man's delight. Heard Lisa Marie and Joey cheer, Grandma Cameron's admiring "That boy can *ride!*"

Dobbin was running out of gas. Chase jammed spurless boot heels into the tiring animal's sides, eliciting a final series of halfhearted jumps. Then the roan broke into a labored lope around the corral.

"Hooray, hooray!" Joey and Lisa Marie, Grandma and Betsy applauded. Ben grinned broadly; Maggie looked relieved.

Only Blair looked exactly as she had from the beginning: white-faced and furious. She, it seemed, hadn't been impressed. Chase slammed the hat back on his head and faced forward in the saddle—just in time to see little Catherine duck under the bottom rail and dash out in front of the lathered horse.

Chase hauled on the reins so hard that Dobbin reared, rising into the air with forelegs flailing. Somebody screamed, but Chase had only the vaguest sense of anyone besides the child, hesitating directly below Dobbin's lethal hooves. Cat looked up with confusion on her face.

There was only one thing Chase could do, and he did it without hesitation; he threw his weight backward and took the horse over with him.

MAGGIE SAW THE MAN she loved pinned beneath twelve hundred pounds of struggling horseflesh and thought she was dying herself. This couldn't be happening! *Let him be all right*, she prayed. *Let him be all right and I promise I'll never come whining to you again.*

Betsy snatched Cat to safety while Maggie and Ben rushed to the fallen horse and rider. Dobbin rolled over and clambered up awkwardly, his hooves flailing as if he had eight, instead of the usual four. The horse trotted a few steps and stopped, legs trembling, sides heaving, but otherwise unhurt.

Chase sat up awkwardly, cursing a blue streak. He saw Ben and waved him off. "Man, I'm sorry. I was showboating, I admit it. I could've killed your little girl, not to mention your horse. Tell me they're both all right."

Maggie and Ben stopped short. Maggie felt as weak with relief as she'd felt with terror.

"They're fine," Ben said. "How about you? Anything busted?"

Chase rolled over onto his hands and knees, then pushed to his feet with a groan. "Nothing hurt but my dignity. It's been a hell of a long time since I got piled like that."

A wide grin split Ben's weathered face. "Let's have it, Britton. Where'd you do your cowboyin'?"

Chase grinned sheepishly. "Montana. My dad thought it'd make a man of me."

"You got a smart father." Ben stuck out his hand. "You're not half-bad yourself. Put 'er there."

They shook. Watching with eyes that watered, Maggie knew the friction between these two men was over for good.

Chase turned toward her, moving cautiously as if he'd been pretty banged up. Before he could say anything, Betsy hurtled into his chest, almost knocking him over.

"Thank you, thank you, thank you!" She kept saying it over and over again. "I should've been watching...."

"Me, too." Grandma Cameron grinned. "Good ridin', boy, and fast thinkin'. You sure showed Dobbin whose old hog eat the cabbage. Next time we want to hoo-raw a tenderfoot, we'll have to find us a new bucker."

Chase enjoyed the approbation, something he'd never expected to earn from this no-bull bunch of rugged individuals. Even Maggie seemed to approve, although she also looked as if she might burst into tears at any moment.

Only Blair seemed unimpressed. Only she had kept her seat atop the corral; only she looked unmoved.

Suddenly it hit him; any further attempts to establish a traditional father-daughter relationship were hopeless. He was never going to get through to her. All he could do was continue making her unhappy.

Her mother wouldn't—couldn't—take her back. Blair was miserable with him. He'd come here today prepared to force her to return to Aspen, make her live with him come hell or high water.

Now he knew he couldn't do that. He couldn't continue making her miserable in the name of love.

Before he could lose his resolve, he took a couple of stiff steps toward her. Looking up into her strained face, he said in a voice that was more like a croak than his usual mellifluous tones, "Okay, Blair, you win. As soon as we get back to Aspen, I'll make the arrangements."

She caught her breath on a little gasp. "What . . . arrangements?"

"To send you to school in Switzerland. You wanted it, you got it."

He'd expected joy and ecstasy, but she just kept staring at him. Then her face began to crumple.

"If I wanted to roller-skate on the freeway, would you let me do that, too?" she shrieked. "I hate you!"

MAGGIE HUGGED the sobbing girl, but she watched Chase. He looked stunned, as if Dobbin had kicked him in the stomach.

"Now what?" He lifted his hat, jammed one hand through his hair and let the hat drop back into place. "No matter what I do, it's wrong."

"It's just your timing," Maggie said. "Blair no longer wants to go to Switzerland, if she ever did. Do you, hon?"

Blair wept harder, clung tighter to Maggie.

"Then what the hell *does* she want?"

"At least one parent who loves her enough to stick with her no matter how obnoxious she gets."

A muffled groan that could have been negative or positive issued from the girl's quivering form.

"I don't get it," Chase said helplessly. "She's acting like this is the ultimate betrayal, when all I was trying to do was make her happy. How plain can I make it? You think it's easy for me to keep coming back when all I get for my efforts is a kick in the teeth? If I could figure out how to make her happy, I'd damn well do it."

Maggie nodded, realizing she knew that more certainly than anyone. Hadn't he proved that when he proposed marriage to a woman he didn't love to provide his daughter with the mother she wanted?

And there it was, the key that had eluded Maggie. Activity around her seemed to freeze into a tableau, and time stood still. She might yet be able to save the day — if she was prepared to bare her humiliation in front of her family and the man she loved. Surely if Blair knew